THE BIG TROUBLE

THE BIG TROUBLE
A WESTERN TRIO

STEVE FRAZEE

SAGEBRUSH
Large Print Westerns

First published in Great Britain by ISIS Publishing Ltd.
First published in the United States by Five Star

Published in Large Print 2011 by ISIS Publishing Ltd.,
7 Centremead, Osney Mead, Oxford OX2 0ES
United Kingdom
by arrangement with
Golden West Literary Agency

British Library Cataloguing in Publication Data
Frazee, Steve, 1909–1992.
    The big trouble.
    1. Western stories.
    2. Large type books.
    I. Title II. Frazee, Steve, 1909–1992. Man who rode
alone. III. Frazee, Steve, 1909–1992. Payroll of the
dead. IV. Frazee, Steve, 1909–1992. Big trouble.
    813.5'4–dc22

ISBN 978–0–7531–8759–3 (pb)

Printed and bound in Great Britain by
T. J. International Ltd., Padstow, Cornwall

Five Star Publishing, a part of Gale, Cengage Learning.

CONTENTS

The Man Who Rode Alone

CHAPTER
ONE

Jim Comstock knew now that he should have ridden away that afternoon, telling Marty Lamb that his outfit was too rank for any man to stomach. Of the ten hardcases facing him at the fire, only moon-faced Slade McQuoin was not on his feet. Seated on a blanket roll near the tailgate of his wagon, the cook merely had reached under the wagon and pulled out a Winchester. It was across his knees, and, like the rest, he looked at Comstock and waited.

Burden George threw the biggest shadow in the roundup camp. He was the ramrod, a powerful, graying man whose belly rode tightly against his gun belt. George did not hurry now that the pot was wide open. Solidly planted, his pale eyes wide and almost mildly questioning, the ramrod shifted his tin cup from right to left hand. He might have been a banker, listening to a plea he could not grant. Deliberately he took a huge swallow of coffee, making a long sucking noise before his lips touched the fluid.

"You're making mighty sudden talk, Comstock," he said.

Across the fire, with his back against the night that carried a chill from the distant Big Horns, Comstock tried to weigh his chances accurately, and the thought persisted that he should have broken his habit of direct honesty and ridden clear when the chance was there, instead of coming in to speak his piece.

"It just come to me this afternoon what this outfit is," he said. He watched Manny Fields edge out to the left, moving to where the firelight died against the night. "Looking for a cinch, Manny?"

There was the one to watch. There was the one with twice the gun skill of Burden George, but Fields would always want the edge. George was hard, direct. He was predictable.

"Just rest them little boots, Manny," the ramrod said. "This ain't no terrible problem." The pale eyes looked across the coffee cup at Comstock. They did not shift and George did not raise his voice when the sounds of Fields's flanking move continued. "I said stand still, Manny."

At the outer edge of the firelight Fields turned his head toward George. White teeth gleamed in his thin dark face as he twisted his mouth in a silent laugh. But he stopped, standing there with his thumbs hooked in his gun belt.

George did not glance at him. "You say you don't like this outfit, Comstock, and you want to quit us."

"I say it ain't my kind of outfit . . . and I'm leaving."

"You were glad enough to get on two days ago."

"That was two days ago."

Comstock looked at Marty Lamb, the friend who had written down to Colorado to say that up here was the chance Comstock had always wanted, an opportunity to start on his own after learning a little about the country. Lamb's expression was a mixture of fear and anger. No shame. Lamb had not always been like that. There was a lot here that Comstock did not know.

George emptied his tin cup and tossed it over his shoulder. It struck a wagon tire and fell to the ground, and then silence came back, broken only by the snap of firewood.

"My leaving won't make any difference," Comstock said. "What you're doing can't be any secret. This is the first range I ever saw where a long-rope crew went out openly with a wagon on roundup."

George smiled briefly. He seemed pleased. "New country, new ways, Comstock. You're young. You can learn a new trick. I was gray before I saw the light."

"I'm leaving."

"I'm not sure about that yet."

He was not playing, Comstock decided. George really had not come to a decision yet.

Manny Fields's voice was like his face, thin and cold. "Too much talk," he said.

Bull Yankton put furrows in his fleshy brow and cheeks as he frowned and nodded. "Yeah," he said.

Over by the wagon Slade McQuoin cleared his throat lightly. His rifle barrel glinted when a little shower of sparks went up from popping wood.

"Beef him," Sioux Chambers said. All the evil in the world seemed gathered in his black eyes and in the bronze lines of a face marked brutally by smallpox.

5

"I dunno," George said. "It's a bet the Association wouldn't send a brand inspector in here." He laughed gently. "What good would it do 'em?"

"Sure they wouldn't!" Lamb said. "I told you I sent for Comstock. We knew he was coming and . . ."

"He's been a long time on the way," Fields said. "Maybe he stopped with the wrong people somewhere. Beef him."

Hackles rose behind the upturned collar of Comstock's blanket jumper, and then for a moment he was apart from all of this, just a spectator watching and listening to a trial beside a campfire. That moment fled and he was studying George again with all the concentration of a man who knew action would stem from the ramrod, even if the first flare was on the fringes.

This was the most brazen, cold-blooded layout he had ever seen. Right at the start he had wondered why they had ridden heavily armed on roundup, but he put that down to the fact that this was rough country, plagued to death by rustlers, as they had told him down in Buffalo on the last lap in.

Every man in the outfit carried a stamp iron and a running iron on his saddle, the stamp iron his own brand, the running iron for venting other brands. There had never been the least pretense of secrecy, and Lamb had let him come to the truth by himself. For two days Comstock had ridden and worked with the boldest rustling crew in existence.

It would have been funny, if he were 200 miles away to talk about it. It was not funny now. They were balancing his life against his death as matter-of-factly as they determined whose turn it was to slap his brand on a maverick.

"He wants to go. Let him go," Lamb said. "He'll leave the country. Won't you, Jim?" Lamb was pleading, now, out of friendship, out of fear, not for himself, but because he had put a friend under the guns of his companions.

"If he rides away from here, he'd better leave the country," George said.

"He ain't riding away from here," Fields said.

McQuoin cleared his throat again. "Ain't we supposed to vote on these things?"

"Sure." Fields nodded. "Beef him."

"Yeah," Bull Yankton said. "Yeah, that's what to do."

"No!" Lamb looked around him wildly.

"Who the hell's running things here?" George asked. "We'll vote one at a time, like human beings. Slade, you keep tally."

"Two ag'in' him, one for him . . . so far," the cook said. "Speak up, boys, one at a time like the boss says."

"Give him to me and Manny," Chambers said.

"Three ag'in' him now." McQuoin was keeping score with his fingers laid across his rifle barrel. "Who's next . . . Ace?"

Ace and Caddo looked at each other. They always rode together. They leaned on each other for decision, Comstock thought. They had been friendly to him, but now he saw no mercy on their fire-lit faces.

Lamb had moved a trifle closer to Burden George. He was trying to tell Comstock something with his

7

eyes. Comstock got it. Lamb would try to take care of the ramrod when the clamp came.

Off to the left Fields's teeth were a silent wolf snarl in the gloom. It would be hard to spot quick movement over there, but Comstock did not intend to wait for the first break.

"Well, Ace?" McQuoin said.

The light ran on Caddo's oily skin. His face was set. He gave Ace a little nod, and then they both looked regretfully at Comstock.

"I guess . . . ," Ace said, and that was all.

Comstock made his draw with the full light on him. He sent the shot toward Manny Fields, and Fields, with all the advantage of gloom, still sought to dodge and draw and fire at the same time. At that, his shot came almost with Comstock's. The bullet seared Comstock's ribs as he turned.

Marty Lamb threw his shoulder hard against George, who cursed him as he tried to draw. The others were slow by a quick breath of time, for they had waited to back a play, not start it. The whip of Fields's second bullet was inches over Comstock's head as he lunged into the gloom, holding low. He flung his body forward, rolling when he hit the ground. Several guns were winking at the outer edges of the light, their owners having leaped away from the fire. Lead smacked the sod and whined into the dark.

Comstock rolled sidewise. He came up on his hands and knees, his six-gun still in his hand. Burden George was still standing in the full light of the fire, with Lamb beside him. The ramrod had drawn his gun, but now he

8

was putting it back into his holster. From the dark where Comstock crouched, George was a clear-cut target.

His voice was scarcely louder than before. "Go after him, boys."

Comstock holstered his gun. He leaped up and ran for the ground-hitched horse he had left 100 feet away from camp, the only precaution he had taken before riding in that night. Two shots went wide. George's voice came a little louder than before.

"I said go after him, you jugheads!"

The *rattle* of a bit when he was already close took Comstock to the horse. A knot slipped through his hand when he grabbed the reins. Even in the heat of savage urgency the knot told him this was not his horse. He sensed, rather than heard, the sound of movement a few feet away.

He had just time to touch his gun, and then the sky fell in on him.

He came back through a world of nausea filled with distant voices that boomed as if in a gigantic cavern. He was on the ground not far from where he had made his break. Yankton was standing over him with a Stetson in his hands.

One of the night guards coming in for coffee, Comstock thought hazily. He had run smack into the man, and the guard must have bent a gun barrel across his head, from the feel of it.

Yankton tipped the hat. Just taking a full breath with his mouth open, Comstock began to strangle when the hatful of water struck him. The coughing put hammers in his head and he was sicker than ever.

Bull slapped the hat back on the deep-crimped shaggy hair. "He's all right, Burden. Better'n he'll ever be again." That tickled Bull. He considered his words, and then he laughed in an experimental way, looking around at the silent dark faces near him. Nobody else laughed.

"Get up," George said. Without looking he used his elbow to jolt Lamb backward when he started to help the injured man. "Save your energy for what you got to do, Marty."

Lamb's face held a sick, trapped expression. He wet his lips and stared at Comstock, who came up to his feet with his head a hell of spinning pain. Things did not clear up very fast. Bull Yankton's deep-wrinkled scowl merged with Sioux Chambers's scarred, bitter face; McQuoin's round features swam past the tortured face of Marty Lamb, and little Manny's thin grimace was everywhere.

Comstock wanted to lean against a wagon wheel and empty his stomach. He staggered, brushing against someone who knocked his arm away savagely.

"You made a poor play, Comstock." George sounded as if he meant it. "Somebody might have got hurt. You lost your sand and ducked too quick."

Strength began to return to Comstock. His vision began to clear. He saw lean, sun-blistered Utah Slim enjoying the coffee that had brought him in from night guard at the wrong moment.

"You should have bluffed it out," George said, "or not left a horse where a man would wonder about it. The vote you couldn't wait for turned out a tie, with me inclined to let you go."

The ramrod let it sink in. Utah Slim made loud work of drinking scalding coffee.

"All right." George made only a small movement with his hand.

Bull and Sioux clamped Comstock's arms across their chests. He was pinned between them, with half his weight off the ground because of Yankton's superior height.

"When you leave," George said, "don't stop this side of Buffalo." Firelight caught his heavy gray sideburns as he turned to Lamb. "All right, Marty. Pay off for that shove you gave me a while ago."

Lamb did not move. The sickness was not only on his face; it was deep inside him. He stared at Comstock until Manny Fields stabbed with the heel of his hand in a vicious shove that sent Lamb stumbling toward Comstock. Lamb stopped. He shook his head, and there was slackness in his lips when he took in a sharp breath that was a groan.

"We can't take all night, Lamb," George said.

Lamb hit Comstock in the face. It was a light blow that skidded off the cheek bone, but it sent hell roaring afresh through Comstock's head.

"We're not playing, Marty," George said. "Get with it, or I'll have Bull take over with those Indian rings of his."

Lamb's next blow was a full swing that snapped Comstock's head against Bull's shoulder. Face clenched in agony, Lamb struck again and again. He was wild, and the slackness of Comstock's body offered no resistance.

"He's trying to knock him out right off!" Fields protested. "Let me do it."

Comstock was insensible to pain now. He knew that his head was jerking when he did not move it, that he could see from one eye only, and that Lamb was trying his best to end it. Marty Lamb, for all his heavy build, had never been much good with his fists. Some said he was muscle-bound.

It ended. Comstock was hanging there between Bull and Sioux, still conscious, his head dropped forward. Through a red mist he saw Lamb's bull-hide chaps move away, and then he saw a tiny pair of boots and heard Fields say: "Hell, he ain't got nearly enough."

CHAPTER
TWO

Anger summoned energy that Comstock hadn't known was in him. He watched the little boots move in. The right one went back a trifle as Fields shifted weight. Comstock brought his leg up and punched with it. He felt the solid impact of his foot smashing into Fields's stomach. The blow flung the little gunman backward and stretched him on the ground.

Comstock spat blood and tried to laugh, but the laugh was short. Bull Yankton chopped down against the side of his neck with a meaty fist, and everything went dark.

In steps that were utter agony Comstock came back to knowing some time later. He was tied belly down across his saddle and the horse was moving slowly through the night. Rain had soaked into his clothes. It was dripping from his face past the bumping stirrup below.

He spoke to the horse. It stopped. His position and his injuries made any kind of movement a hellish thing, but after a time he worked his hands free of the water-slackened rope. It fell away under the belly of the horse and he was able to kick his feet loose. He tried to twist his way upright in the saddle, but when his head came up, blackness smote him like a blow and he slipped from the rig.

The horse shied away. He tried to crawl through the wet grass and catch a stirrup, but the horse was cold and nervous. It leaped aside, and then trotted briskly into the darkness, and Comstock was alone in the night, with the rain soaking into his tortured body. His hat was gone. He had last seen his gun in Slade McQuoin's hands when the cook was examining it.

For a while he sat on the ground with his head on his knees, until the waves of pain and nausea began to lessen. Then he rose and began to walk through the rain-sodden night. Except for the country he had ridden during his two days with the rustler crew, he knew nothing about this range. Lamb had met him on a trail not far north of Buffalo, and they had not passed a ranch on their way in. Stumbling through the darkness, Comstock knew now why Lamb had avoided ranches.

Dawn found him sitting on a rolling hill, with nothing but other rolling hills around him. The rain had stopped. He rose and took off his jumper, with the thought of whipping some of the water from it. The garment was split under the arms and up the middle of the back to the collar, rent from his struggling while Bull and Sioux held him.

Comstock fought sodden flannel back into the twisted blanket lining and went wearily down the hill. One hill became another. The sun came out hotly and pounded at his head. He crossed a little gully where longhorns at a water hole flung up their heads and challenged him. Ordinarily he would have been wary of them, but now he stumbled straight ahead and cursed the cattle. They broke and hightailed.

It was afternoon when he went over another hill just like countless others, and saw a roundup wagon near a stream below. A long-legged man was asleep or resting on blanket rolls, with his back against a wagon wheel, a rifle close at hand. If the man had been napping, he was not asleep when Comstock came closer.

Sharp blue eyes surveyed Comstock. The man rose unhurriedly. He was long in the legs, long in the middle, and his neck was long. He was six inches taller than Comstock, straight as a stretched rope, with a lean brown face that showed a half dozen cut marks from recent shaving.

Without a word he poured coffee from a pot on the coals of a fire. He pushed the cup toward Comstock and kicked a bedroll closer to him.

After the third cup Comstock began to feel half alive. He observed a pistol brand burned into the side of the wagon, and the same mark on horses picketed downwind from the camp.

The tall cook came back from the fire with a tin plate of beans and warmed-up biscuits with sorghum poured over them. Comstock cleaned the plate. He wiped it out with grass and put it on the cook board of the wagon. The man handed him the makings.

Those sharp blue eyes did not miss much, Comstock thought. He nodded his thanks when he returned the tobacco. He had taken his second drag when he saw the three riders galloping toward the camp.

The first one was on an enormous bay that shone red-gold in the sun. Even at a distance the darkness of the rider's face contrasted sharply with his white hat. He rode like a cavalryman, instead of a cowboy, Comstock thought. A little closer, and Comstock was sure of his first guess, the bay was a stallion, and a beauty.

Dismounting at the fire, two of the riders picked up cups and watched Comstock critically. The dark-faced man came on, swinging down when he was close to the wagon. The inquiry of deep-set gray eyes went over Comstock with hard directness. The man was big and solid, with the hardness that comes from long hours in the saddle. His manner said he owned this outfit and the grass he stood on.

He said to the cook: "Move the wagon on up to the head of Medicine Creek, Sky Joe. Make it in time for supper."

The cook began to load bedrolls without a word. One of the riders at the fire gulped hastily at his coffee and went after the horses. The dark-faced man turned on Comstock.

"What the devil are you doing here?"

"I stopped to eat."

"Now you've eaten." The man took in half the compass with an arm motion.

"You own this Pistol outfit?" Comstock asked.

"I'm Major Collins." That implied ownership of Pistol and half of Wyoming. "Better ride, cowboy."

"I lost my horse."

"Too bad. Walking's good, though."

Anger stemming from a good many things put its heat into Comstock. "What's your point, Collins?"

"You came here with Marty Lamb. You went to work for Burden George two days back. Now git!"

"I didn't know what I was getting into at the time."

Collins laughed. "Get off Pistol range. Walk or crawl, whatever suits you best. Tell George he must be getting soft in the head, trying to run a spy in on me."

"I never asked you for anything."

"And don't."

When men like Collins got an idea, it sat like a rock in their heads, Comstock thought. His anger over an entire situation was now focused on the Pistol owner, but he held his temper and tried again. "I came in here when Lamb sent for me, that's true, but I thought it was an honest deal. When I found out it wasn't, George and the rest gave me a little trouble about leaving."

"It took you two full days to find out?" Collins laughed.

"That was fair time, considering this is the first range I ever saw where rustlers have the Indian sign on cowmen so bad they can put a wagon out at roundup." Comstock drove the insult as deep as he could by making it soft and slow.

The Pistol owner's eyes went down to slits. He took a deep breath and held it. Sky Joe stood motionlessly, his face without expression. The second cowboy, who had come over to help load the wagon, looked quickly from his boss to Comstock, then gently laid on the ground the bedroll he was lifting.

"I'd slap that down your throat . . . if you didn't look half dead already," Collins said.

"I'm on my feet. I cover the ground I stand on."

Collins shook his head slowly. "A beat-up cripple. No gun, either. Go back to Burden George and his murdering crew. Tell George his little play won't work with Major Collins." The Pistol owner turned away. He swung up on the stallion with easy grace. "Come on, boys. Get that wagon rolling, Sky Joe."

The three riders went galloping up the creek, Collins in the lead, bumping like a cavalryman.

Sky Joe tossed up the remaining bedrolls and climbed to the wagon seat.

Comstock grinned wryly, and the movement hurt his battered mouth. "Thanks for the grub, Sky Joe." He turned to walk away.

"Wait." It was the first word the cook had spoken. It rolled out with a thump, like heavy liquid from a jug.

"Take the buckskin." There was a wiry gelding tied behind the wagon. "It's mine," Sky Joe said, when he saw the hesitation in Comstock's eyes. He reached behind the seat and tossed a six-gun down to Comstock. "Go west to Anvil Creek. Yellow gravel all along the bottom. Go up it. The Star B's near the head. That's mine." He spat. "Nobody there."

Comstock blinked. "You own a ranch?"

"Slade McQuoin owns a ranch, almost as good as mine. Still he slings grub for a rustler crew. Lamb owns a ranch, too."

Erect in the springless seat, his long neck as stiff as his back, Sky Joe spoke to the horses and drove away.

18

A blamed funny country, Comstock thought.

He rode west on the buckskin. It was fifteen miles, at least, to Anvil Creek. The sun was getting long when he came to it and let the gelding drink above bright yellow gravel. He had seen several hundred steers in scattered bunches, and two riders at a distance. Used to the mountain-bound ranges of Colorado, Comstock began to appreciate the vastness that served both cattlemen and rustlers up here.

Along the creek he saw the evidence of heavy grazing, but he ran into only a half dozen stragglers as he rode upstream. They bore the brands of three different outfits, but none was Star B.

Before long he knew that the bottom had been cleared of cattle by two riders, who had driven them upstream. He grew more puzzled when the tracks did not turn toward the low ridges that bounded both sides of the valley. Sky Joe had said there was nobody at Star B, but if the ranch house was near the head of the stream . . .

The creek went into long strings of beaver ponds, and above them it began to dwindle.

Comstock swung off behind the west ridge. He was on foot when he looked down on the ranch house. There were two large pole corrals and a smaller one behind them. The larger ones were full of cattle. Over a gate that led into a grassy yard hung a sign of peeled willows that formed a star.

Struggling at his gun belt, a stocky man came from the main building. He walked around the corrals, stood

19

a moment scanning the ridges, then returned to the house.

There was a horseshoe of thick timber behind the buildings. Comstock considered it thoughtfully. Then he decided to ride straight in. That was the surest way of finding out what was going on at a ranch that the owner had said was vacant.

He hailed when the buckskin was still fifty yards from the gate. Two men came out. One looked like the other, red of face, red-headed. They stood apart from each other in the yard and waited tensely.

Comstock went in from the gate on foot, towing the buckskin loosely.

He got close enough to see wiry whisker stubble, and that was close enough for them to see his beaten features.

"That's him! Look at that face!"

The one who spoke should not have talked, and his partner should not have taken time to listen before going for his gun. It made the difference of a fraction.

The speaker had his pistol clear of leather when Comstock's bullet hit him in the heart. The second man got off a shot that fanned Comstock's cheek and struck the saddle. Comstock hurried his own shot too much. It went a little high and wide, taking the second redhead in the shoulder. The impact knocked the man flat on his back.

Comstock went over and kicked his gun away, but there was no need. The man was gray and dazed from shock. It was several minutes before he staggered to his

20

feet. He held his shoulder and looked down at his dead companion.

He cursed in a shaking voice. "You killed Pete!"

"I tried to do the same for you."

"You lousy Association spy!"

"You got the wrong word pretty fast."

The wounded man was still sick from shock, but he snarled like a cornered wolf and his green eyes sparked defiance. "Comstock, you'd better kill me, too . . . right now! Because when I get you dead to rights, I won't be soft like Burden George!"

"You rustlers got a good communications system, ain't you?" Comstock picked up the two guns. In the house he found two long guns that had come from the boots of two saddles on the floor. He left them all inside and went back to the wounded man.

"Shall I look at your shoulder?"

"To hell with you!"

"Suit yourself."

Comstock took the man with him and made him sit on the ground while Comstock saddled the two horses in the small corral.

A little later the fellow rode away, going west, his right hand thrust into his jumper front for support. He towed the horse with Pete's body lashed across the saddle. He had made one threat; he made no more in leaving.

Comstock released the cattle. There were eight different brands in all, about a third Pistol. No Star B stuff. Apparently Sky Joe did not own a cow.

The sun died quickly. Comstock felt his face and looked thoughtfully in the direction the redhead had gone.

There was a saddle of fresh beef in the kitchen. The two had eaten and left their dirty utensils where they last used them. Comstock cleaned up the mess and cooked himself a steak two inches thick. One was good, and so he had another with a second pot of coffee. He hung the meat in a flour sack on a roof pole behind the house, and tidied up the kitchen with the thoroughness of one settling for a long stay.

Just at dark he picketed the buckskin in a small park in the trees north of the house. Taking blankets and the two rifles, he bedded down at the edge of the timber where the east wing of the horseshoe came to the grass.

Buildings and corrals merged with the darkness. Coyotes began to yap and howl on the ridges. Down the valley, the cattle he had turned loose bawled complaints as they settled down for the night.

Comstock was asleep in five minutes.

It was blacker than a lobo's mouth when the whickering of the buckskin roused him. With a rifle across his knees he sat listening. The deeper tone of a wolf scattered the yapping of coyotes down the valley, and then silence held once more. For a long ten minutes Comstock waited, and nothing came but night sounds that were familiar.

Yet he knew that things were not right. He waited another five minutes before slipping on his boots, and then he went into the open and stood listening. After a while, frowning at the feel of a night that seemed so natural, he went toward the house, moving carefully, somewhat stiffly because of muscles abused the night before.

He went across the grassy yard, straining to catch the sound of movement anywhere near the corrals. A circle of the outbuildings brought him nothing but the *squeak* of field mice in a shed. He was almost to one corner of the house when he tensed and raised the rifle instinctively.

A flick of light had winked from the kitchen window, just a tiny flare that came and died and left an afterglow before his eyes. Someone had struck a match in there.

Close to the corner of the house he stopped and waited. Footsteps came from the kitchen toward the front door. One man, walking lightly. There might be a dozen more somewhere out in the blackness. Comstock had to know.

He laid the rifle on the grass and moved in closer.

Without hesitation the man came through the door. By the tone of his boot sounds, one solidly on the narrow plank porch, the second muffled as it struck ground, Comstock had the fellow's position exactly.

Comstock's left arm went out and came in. The crook of his elbow slammed into the man's throat and tightened hard to shut off outcry. His right hand went down and slapped a holster, and then he cleared the gun and tossed it to one side. It was quick and easy. And then he had a tall handful of hell.

A head came back and cracked his swollen lips. The fellow drove a sharp boot heel into his instep. Elbows beat a tattoo on his ribs. He cinched in with his left arm.

"Lay off . . . or I'll tear your head loose," he growled.

Dragging the man with him, he backed to the door. The fellow was quiet now, almost limp. Comstock listened a moment. The struggle had been sharp and quick, with not much carrying noise. He backed the rest of the way inside.

"I'm letting the pressure off. Keep your voice down and I won't break . . ." He released all the pressure. "Good God!"

He had put his face down close to whisper, and jammed it into a mass of hair that carried a faint scent. Almost too late he sensed the tensing of the woman he had trapped. He grabbed her arm as she sprang toward the door. She pulled him a step forward with the surge before he could drag her back.

"Lay off! I don't want to hurt you!"

She hit him in the face three times. They would not have been blows to make him blink ordinarily, but now they hurt plenty. The sharp heel stamped down again, two vicious drives that struck almost where the first had bruised his instep. Comstock had his choice of smothering this wildcat or knocking her kicking. He reached out to haul her in.

She drove the heel of her free hand into his face. It jammed under his swollen nose and blinded him with pain. She jerked away and was out of the room while he was still groping for her. Comstock heard her speeding across the yard. She went toward the timber north of the house.

Blinking moisture from his eyes, he thought: *The devil with her. Let her go.* It would have been better if he had caught a man.

The buckskin neighed not long afterward, and then Comstock heard a horse in the timber, going toward the east ridge. He picked up his rifle and went back to his blankets. No matter how he tried to ease his left foot, there was throbbing agony in it, and every time he dozed fitfully and rubbed the blankets across his nose, he jerked away and came awake. A man was a fool to stay in a country where redheads drew on sight, and women sneaked by night to beat your face to a pulp.

CHAPTER
THREE

At daylight he went to the buckskin in the little park. Tracks showed that the woman had come directly to the gelding, left her mount, and gone to the house on foot. Comstock shook his head. He made a careful circle through the timber and on the open ridges above it. No one but the redheads and the woman had come or gone in the last week.

Between him and the Big Horns there was no sign that man had ever ventured into this country. On the rolling, grassy hills it was the same in all other directions. For a long moment Comstock was homesick for Colorado, where a man had his bearings all the time.

He went back to the house. From what he had seen of the Star B, it would be a going concern — if there were any cattle belonging to it. Sky Joe must have had cattle once.

In the yard he picked up the gun he had lifted last night. A .38 pistol, especially built on a light frame, five cartridges in it. He took it inside and hung it on a peg. He was getting a fine collection of iron, at least. In the kitchen he looked into a mirror over the washstand. A fine collection of lumps that would make him a holy horror at any hoe-down, that is, if any of the savages up here ever took time out for such things.

He was here. He had left the savings of ten years in a Cheyenne bank on his way up. That had been the one smart thing he had done, after taking Marty Lamb's word that here was a country where a man could get a start. He was going to stay here — at least until he heard from long Sky Joe. Let rustlers or anyone else try to blast him out of the Star B until he was ready to go.

No one blasted him. They caught him flat-footed in the middle of the afternoon.

He was at the little corral, currying the buckskin, when he saw the four riders coming up the valley. Major Collins's red-gold stallion was in the lead, beside a long-legged black.

Comstock put up the bars, took his rifle, and started toward the house, watching over his shoulder.

He did not see the two men who came around the back of the house with rifles until it was too late.

"Drop it, Comstock."

They were the same two who had ridden into the Pistol camp with Collins the day before.

Comstock dropped his rifle.

"Now the gun belt . . . and do it easy like."

Comstock obeyed. "Nice country," he murmured.

One of the riders leaned his rifle against his belt buckle and rolled a smoke while waiting for Collins to come up.

The rider of the shining black was a woman, tall in her rig, straight as Sky Joe himself. She was the first woman Comstock had ever seen who wore hair cut to

27

shoulder length. It was as black as the horse she rode. Her eyes were dark, her face somewhat long, with a dusky undertone.

They did raise something in Wyoming besides hell, Comstock told himself. His eyes narrowed when he saw she wore a gun. From where he stood it looked like a .38.

Collins rested both hands on the apple and looked down with a satisfied expression. "You search him?"

One of the men behind Comstock said: "No, Major, but . . ."

"Search him, you fool!"

That was done. Collins swung down. The two riders behind him dismounted, and one took a yearling hide from his cantle strings. The woman rode on toward the house, not even glancing at Comstock as she passed.

"You don't know when you're well off, do you, Comstock?" the Pistol owner asked.

"You're off your range, Collins. Nobody invited you here, or asked you to get off your horse. If you got anything to say, speak out and ride."

Collins blinked. His mouth hung open in the act of closing on a cigar. "Well, by God!" Then anger began to gather in the deep-set gray eyes. He reached back and grabbed the yearling hide from the man who held it. The hide dragged a messy way across the fellow's jumper and one part whipped up and struck him in the face, but Collins did not notice.

"You can read that brand, can't you, Comstock?"

Collins held the hide spread out. It was Pistol.

"I can read it," Comstock said.

28

"Uhn-huh. Not quite as stupid as you look." Collins jerked his head at one of the men behind Comstock. "Find the meat around here some place, Buck."

"On a roof pole at the back of the cabin," Comstock said. "I didn't kill it."

Collins made a short sound. He lit his cigar, and took time to glance around the Star B with shrewd interest.

Comstock looked over his shoulder. The woman was coming out of the house. She turned her head toward the west ridge and Comstock caught a glimpse of a broad red mark of irritation on her throat. His eyes darted to the wrinkled fabric of his jumper where it lay in deep bends at the elbow.

She came back to the group, and she did not glance at Comstock. From the front of her open shirt collar the red mark was not so apparent, but he saw it clearly as she passed at his side.

Buck returned with the sack of meat. Collins grew irritated at his efforts to strip the covering. He snatched it from his rider's hands and ripped the flour sack.

"That look like yearling to you?" Collins thrust the meat at Comstock.

"Uhn-huh."

Collins dropped the meat on the ground beside the fresh hide. "They go together?"

"Probably."

"Wherever you come from, Comstock . . . what do they do with rustlers?"

"The first thing they don't do is let 'em go out on roundup with the cowmen. Now and then somebody beefs a yearling to eat." Comstock spoke with exaggerated slowness. He did not need sarcasm; he let a thin smile serve. "But if we happened to have gangs branding everything that moved, we wouldn't take our full crew out to sneak in on a man who had killed just one scrubby yearling."

Collins's dark face paled. He clamped the cigar so hard it drooped. His voice grated up from fury. "You admit, then, you beefed a Pistol yearling?"

"No, I don't admit it. In fact, I didn't do it. The meat was in the house when I got here. Two red-headed jaspers were making themselves to home. The corrals were full of stuff they probably intended to move today."

"That's right, Major," Buck said.

The deep-set eyes came up in a wicked stare. "What's right? How do you know?"

"About the cattle, I mean," Buck said. He was a gangling blond youngster, and his face showed how much he resented his employer's harsh question, as well as his own error in not making himself clear the first time. "You can see the tracks where somebody . . ."

"I saw the tracks, you idiot! Comstock and two of his brother rustlers had the stuff here . . . and then they had to let go fast."

"I don't see why," Buck said stubbornly. "Them tracks was all made yesterday. If they was figuring . . ."

"Comstock, this range can't stand any more men like you," Collins said. He had gone from prosecutor to judge, and now he had to make a little speech to prove to himself that he was right. "You tried to run a sandy on me yesterday. You talked one of my employees into quitting me at a critical time. Then you moved in at Star B, rustled cattle, killed one of my yearlings . . ."

"You've got horseshoes in your head, Collins. If your men quit you, I'm for 'em. They're smart. As far as rustling or killing beef, I told you once two red-headed fellows . . ."

Collins spat out his cigar. His eyes had a metallic sheen. "The evidence is in. Comstock, you're guilty." He motioned to the men behind him. "Hang him, boys."

The woman spoke calmly. "No, we'll have no hanging. I'm inclined to believe his story."

Buck bobbed his head. "Me, too, Major. I think . . ."

"Damn your thinking, Skelton! I've had enough of your lip!" Collins looked at the woman. "You get on that horse, Caroline, and wait down the valley."

"I'll go nowhere," the woman said. "You're not . . ."

"Then stay! I hope it makes you sick!" Collins was trembling with rage. "Hang him, boys."

One of the riders behind Collins began taking a rope from his saddle. When he had it in his hands, he hesitated, his face set and pale. "Maybe . . ."

"You heard me!" Collins said.

The rider braced himself. "Hell's fire, just a rustler," he muttered. He started forward, and the two beside him took the cue from his determination.

Comstock had his position gauged. The man standing at his back with Buck was holding his rifle a trifle high. Comstock intended to drive in low and bowl the man over, taking a chance on Buck. After that . . . well, they were not going to hang Jim Comstock.

"Rope him where he stands," Collins ordered.

"Leave him where he stands!" The deep voice rolled out from the corner of the house. Sky Joe was there, with a rifle laid across a log. "Drop the rope, Bundy."

The rope went down on the grass in a yellow coil.

"Collins gets it in the belly at the first wrong move. Get clear, Comstock."

With the heat fully on him, Collins smiled. "You've thrown in with 'em, eh, Sky Joe?"

Holding low so he would not cover any of the group, Comstock scooped up his rifle and six-gun belt, and got off to the side.

"Ride out," Sky Joe ordered the group. "Stay clear of Star B grass, unless you're riding up like men, instead of sneaking murderers."

"You've put the brand on yourself, Sky Joe!" Collins shouted. He whirled toward his horse.

Comstock said: "Hold up a minute, Buck."

The blond youth turned with a surprised look. The rest stopped to watch and listen.

"How would you like to work for a white man for a change?" Comstock asked.

Buck blinked. He was young enough that his thinking was not rutted. The idea caught and stuck and spread across his face in a grin. "You're on!"

"The whelp . . . throwing in with rustlers," Collins snarled.

"Sky Joe backed this," Buck said. "He ain't no rustler. We all know that."

"He is now." Collins went up and sent the stallion away with a lunge.

Caroline was the last to leave. She gave Comstock a long slow look before she mounted the black. He was quite sure of the red mark on her throat as she turned away. She rode off unhurriedly, smoothing her divided skirt as she went under the Star B sign.

"Where does she fit?" Comstock asked.

Buck gave him a surprised look. "Why, she's the daughter of the old Collins hellion."

She should not be prowling around bachelor ranches at night, then, Comstock thought. He turned to grin at Sky Joe.

Over a pot of coffee, Comstock and Sky Joe sat in the kitchen and compared notes. Buck was scouting the ridges.

"We can look for trouble from Pug Ellis and his boys anytime," Sky Joe said. He stretched long legs halfway across the room. "I didn't take you for a gunman."

"I'm not."

"You got Pete Ellis and stopped Pug."

"Luck, mainly."

Sky Joe grunted. "Their outfit . . . Pug's now . . . is just as tough as Burden George's."

"How many rustler layouts are on this range?"

"Four, five . . . that run wagons."

Comstock looked out the window at grass where no Star B cows grazed. "They clean you out?"

"Not at first. Big cattlemen squeezed me dry. The long-ropes just took the leavings."

"Collins?"

"He was one."

"That sort of thing helps make rustlers," Comstock said.

"Yep. Cattlemen played freeze-out with Burden George and Slade McQuoin, others. Marty Lamb, too."

"Now you got more long-ropes than cowmen?"

"About," Sky Joe grunted. "And Pistol."

Comstock inhaled his smoke slowly. "You quit Collins. Now you aiming to start again?"

Sky George nodded. "Been aiming to do so for years. I just slid along, like others. Some cleared out. George, Lamb, some more went the other route."

"Why didn't you?"

"Don't rightly know. Why'd you quit George when you got things straight?"

"Some things a man can't take."

"Yep," Sky Joe said. "It's the way he's made." The lean man stared out the window. "Aside from that, there'll be law here someday. Them as last and come out of it with good holdings will be the ones that went with what's right now."

Sky Joe was silent a long time. The coffee pot *thumped* on the stove. In the small corral the buckskin and a little sorrel mare Sky Joe had led out of the timber grunted as they took a dust bath.

"You come staggering in," Sky Joe said. "Half dead, beat to a pulp. If you'd been carried on a shutter, you'd've looked better. No whining. No complaints. I figured what happened before you talked to Collins. It ain't the first time George and them others showed how they don't like a man to quit. It struck me. I'd been figuring a long time I ought to fight instead of run. The way Collins acted finished me. I meant to stay the roundup, but when he roared about me giving you the buckskin, I told him what to do with his spread."

Sky Joe was studying Comstock. There was something in the calm, level expression that reminded the younger man of Caroline Collins.

"I got land," Sky Joe said. "I got twenty-two legal-held sections on this crick, and all the range I'm man enough to hold. Fight it out with me, Comstock, and it's half yours."

Comstock stared. "That's a liberal offer to a man you don't know."

"I size up a man quick. Fifty percent of the time I make a whale of a mistake. Well, it's only fifty percent of the ranch I'm offering, and maybe we both got a fifty percent chance to live long enough to enjoy it."

Comstock considered. "You're on. I've got some money . . ."

"We won't need it. We'll build our stock from mavericks. Nothing wrong in that." Sky Joe cocked his head.

Comstock shook his head. "We buy our stuff, or I'm not in it."

Sky Joe's long face was somber. "Glad you said that. We'll pay our way . . . and fight when paying ain't enough."

CHAPTER
FOUR

For a while Comstock sat looking from the window, his mind leaping over all immediate problems, seeing the Star B as it could be. It was a pretty picture.

"What's the governor think about the situation up here?" Sky Joe asked casually.

"The governor? How do I know?" The sharp blue eyes studied Comstock a long time. "I'll take your word on that. Collins wouldn't."

"Did Collins think I . . . ?"

"Right from the first. Some of the smaller ranchers have been after the governor for years to do something up here. It's headed up now to where some folks think maybe he *is* investigating. You looked like a likely man for the job."

"Collins knows I came in with Marty Lamb."

"Lamb was one of the small ranchers that asked the governor for help . . . that is, until a while back when he got plumb disgusted and joined up with George's crew." Sky Joe cleared his throat. "You come here with the wrong man, Comstock. George's crew ain't none too strong on Lamb. He switched sides once, not that I blame him much. He could switch again."

"Lamb knows I'm not from the governor."

"Him and me. Who else?"

"Uhn-huh. Then that's maybe why Collins wanted to string me high."

"That's why. There's some cool heads with Burden George, and they kept it from being a straight-out killing because they don't want the territory to heat up and send in the militia. The Ellis boys wouldn't have stopped to consider. Collins had a better chance. You got to admit the evidence of that beef and hide was all against you. Brother, Collins had you set up to roll. He would have bulled it through and allowed afterward that maybe he made a mistake." Sky Joe filled the coffee cups again. "Yes, sir, I size a man up quick. Biggest mistake I ever made was on Collins. I sized him A-One before we come out here together. We was pardners. When Pistol got man-size, I found myself on the outside, gawping like a fish out of water, saying . . . 'What happened?' It was all nice and legal. I took up Star B. Every time one of my cows got a foot out of this valley, it was on Pistol range. That was anywhere from the Big Horns to the Missouri River, maybe farther. Collins never set no limits. My cattle had trouble. Some got shot. I had to catch a calf a-borning to get Star B on it before a Pistol brand beat me. So help me, I think some of my cows had calves with Pistol on 'em before they was borned. I couldn't keep no riders. They got a bad habit of getting themselves shot. In them days the rustlers hardly ever touched Pistol stuff. Some said Collins had an agreement with 'em." Sky Joe waved his hand. "Pretty soon the small ranches had grass growing in their yards." He shook his head. "Hell, man, I've done a year's talking in the last few minutes. You finish it."

"All right. The rustlers outgrew their pants. Every small spread that went down made more long-ropes, so the wild crews were big enough to take Pistol stuff or anything they wanted. Collins can stand the loss of cattle right now, considering he's gunning for the whole country. He gets that, and then he's the damnedest enemy the rustlers ever had. In the end, they can't win. He can."

"You got it," Sky Joe said.

Comstock grinned. "Maybe we better raise hogs here. Ever hear of anyone rustling hogs?"

Sky Joe's grin split his lean face and took years off him. He wasn't very old at that, Comstock thought, maybe in his late forties.

"Yeah, we could keep all the calf hogs . . . baby hogs, whatever they are . . . under the bunk, and every morning we could vent the Pistol brands that appeared during the night. I tell you, Comstock, Pistol don't even need running irons. They get their mark on everything by some kind of thought wave."

Sky Joe sat grinning for a while, but pretty soon his face fell back into somber lines.

He asked: "Caroline pull a gun on you when she found you here last night?"

Comstock's eyes swung quickly. "How'd you know she was here?"

"I cut her sign in the little park where she always leaves her horse. When I'm here, she comes by frequent. When I ain't, she drops by now and then to keep an eye on things."

Comstock told him what had happened the night before.

"She should have knowed you was a friend, after she seen the buckskin."

"I didn't act much like a friend," Comstock said. "It would have been bad if she came earlier, when the Ellis boys were here."

Sky Joe shook his head. "They wouldn't have bothered her. She rides the whole range, rustler spreads and all."

"She might have bothered them." Comstock felt his nose. "She blamed near wrecked me. What does her old man think about her coming here?"

"It galls him bitter. You saw her. What can he do? If he ever does try to get rough with Caroline, I'll kill him. I've told him so." The blue eyes glittered like ice chips. "I can overlook Collins's stealing me blind and making a cook outta me, but I won't stand flat-footed if he ever touches that girl. She's my dead twin sister's girl, you see."

The bleakness of Sky Joe's tone and expression lay heavily in the room. Comstock was silent.

Sky Joe cocked his head suddenly. "There's our crew . . . and he's coming in lickety-brindle!"

They were at the front door before Comstock heard the horse in the timber. Buck Skelton was moving fast, sure enough.

Comstock picked up a rifle and checked the loads. He was reaching for another rifle when he noticed a .38

he did not remember on the peg where he had hung the one he took from Caroline. This was a standard job. The especially built pistol was gone. She had made the exchange when she went into the house a while before.

Protruding from the barrel was a piece of paper that read when opened:

Pistol plans to burn Star B tonight.

Comstock passed the note to Sky Joe.

The tall man's face showed no emotion. "Trouble," he said, "is like mud. It comes in gobs."

Buck came in on the run and leaped down. "Six men coming in from the west. I recognized Bill Indio's gray gelding."

Sky Joe grinned at Comstock. "Indio is Pug Ellis's toughest lad. How come, Comstock, in two, three days you got everybody in Wyoming gunning for you?"

"They're not pushing themselves . . . but they'll get here just the same." For a moment Buck looked as if he wished he had stayed with Pistol.

"They think I'm here alone," Comstock said. "Let's do this . . ." After he stated the plan, he looked at Sky Joe. "They never bothered you, huh?"

"Nope. Just stole my cows, and used Star B as a roundup point when I was away. Never bothered me none."

The four riders came straight off the west ridge, skirting the timber. They crossed the creek in a rush, came through the gate the same way, and then they spread out widely in the yard. If Burden George's crew was hard, this group was just a little harder, Comstock thought. He was in the harness shed, watching through a crack.

Indio, on a chunky gray, was a stringy, hawk-faced man who looked like he would not trust his own mother. He did the talking when Sky Joe stepped from the door.

"Where's the fellow that gunned Pete Ellis?"

Sky Joe was cradling a Winchester. "Fair fight, I hear. Pug and Pete had good odds."

"You trying to get salty . . . after all these years, Long Joe? Where's this Comstock?"

Comstock would have stepped out then, but he had not yet spotted the two other rustlers. They probably were in the edge of the timber, covering the back of the house. He hoped Buck had sense enough to take off his boots before trying to come in at their backs.

"Yep, I'm getting salty," Sky Joe said. "Star B is resuming business."

One of the mounted men laughed. He was a thin blade of a man and he reminded Comstock of Manny Fields in a way. "Get good stuff this time, Sky Joe. Some of the scrubs you had last time wasn't hardly worth the taking."

"Shut up, Dandy." Indio's face was like a bronze hatchet. "Last time, Sky Joe . . . where's this Comstock?"

"You see one horse in the corral, don't you?" Sky Joe was stalling. The plan called for Comstock to start the play.

But he did not want to open the pot until he had at least an idea of where the last two rustlers were. He could not see a sign in the timber. It would be bad if they had swung clear around to come in from the east.

"Maybe the guy did slope, Indio," one of the riders said. "If what we heard about him and Collins . . ."

"Collins couldn't scare a nervous steer with a barrel of gunpowder." Indio raised a little higher in the saddle. His left hand took in slack on the reins. His right hand went back for a quick drop to his gun. "Dandy, you and Jake go through the house."

"Them days are gone," Sky Joe said. "Don't nobody swing down unless he figures to stay in this valley."

Dandy had one foot out of the stirrup. "By God, he means it, Indio."

"Get down, Dandy!" Indio said.

Comstock still had not spotted the last two of the six, but he could not wait any longer. He stepped from the shed when there was daylight between Dandy's pants and his saddle.

"Over here, Indio."

"It's him!" somebody said.

Indio said nothing. His right hand went down. But he was caught from the flank and had to twist in the saddle. Even then, if Comstock had not dropped to his knees, he would have been center drilled by the lightning shot that crashed the weathered boards behind him. He aimed deliberately and shot Bill Indio sidewise from the saddle.

Sky Joe's timing was exact. The instant all heads turned toward Comstock, the tall man began pumping lead into the horses. He had said when the plan was made that the thought of killing a man always sickened him, so now he shot the horses.

Comstock took aim at slender Dandy, who had fought his horse to control. A screaming mount reared high and came between the front sight and the target just as Comstock pulled the trigger. The horse went down. Its rider was flung sidewise and lost his gun. Dandy was taking cold aim at Sky Joe in the instant when Comstock was working the rifle lever. He knew he was too late to help his partner.

A rifle blasted from the timbers behind the house. Dandy jerked. He bent across the pommel, hanging on with both hands, and then he fell loosely to the ground.

It was over then. Dandy and Indio were dead. Their two companions had been thrown, bruised but sound. They stood with sullen awe on their faces when Comstock and Sky Joe walked forward. Buck came out of the timber, hobbling barefooted, driving two more men before him.

"Look at that!" Sky Joe cursed bitterly, pointing to the brand on a wounded blue roan on the ground. "My own horse, stole over a year ago. And they never even bothered to vent the Star B!"

He put the animal out of its misery. Two others were dead. Bill Indio's gray gelding had run to the back end of a corral, unhurt.

Buck came up with his two prisoners. His fair face was deathly pale. He would not look at Dandy. He stammered when he said: "I . . . I thought I was going to miss that shot. It was like something done real slow."

Comstock knew just how he felt. "Sky Joe's got a bottle in the cupboard, Buck. Go get a drink."

Buck started, then came back. "No. No, I ain't taking no whiskey to help make me think something's right . . . when I already know it's right."

Comstock looked the prisoners over. One of the pair that Buck had surprised was no older than Skelton, and it seemed to Comstock that the fellow didn't yet have the deep marks of the wild bunch in the set of his face.

"How long've you been with the Ellis boys?" Comstock asked.

"A month. It was the only job I could get up here."

"Want to switch?"

The youth was more scared than he had ever been before. He licked his lips and stared at Comstock's battered face, and then he shot a quick look at his sullen fellow captives, and lastly he looked at the two dead men.

"Go ahead and switch, Button," one of the prisoners said. "But don't ever ride out of the yard, if you do."

Comstock watched the lad, and gave him no help. He saw what he wanted to see when Button's face tightened, and he gave the other rustlers a steady look. "To hell with you. I'm quitting. Do what you think you can do about it!"

Sky Joe rubbed his long chin and muttered: "Fifty percent of the time . . . I hope you have better luck than me, Comstock."

Comstock turned to the other rustlers. "Clear out. Take Dandy and Indio with you. You got one horse to carry 'em. We're keeping the gray in exchange for that dead blue roan with Star on it."

44

"You're salty, all right," one of the rustlers said. "But you ain't going to be salty enough, Comstock."

Comstock took Buck's pistol and laid it on the ground. "Threats and guts don't go together. Pick up the pistol, friend."

Fear rode in an ugly wave across the rustler's face. "Naw, you don't! You don't trap me that way, the whole bunch of you!" It was not the "whole bunch" he was afraid of. He knew it, and he could see that everyone else knew it, and that knowledge made him as deadly an enemy as Comstock could ever create.

Six had come in on Star B. Three walked away, towing a horse that carried the bodies of two more.

Sky Joe cocked his head. "That just about wrecks the Ellis gang."

Comstock knew what he was thinking. The Ellis crew was only one of many, and then there was Collins and the other big ranchers, if they were as grasping as the Pistol owner. And immediately, there was the matter of which Caroline had warned. It would be a long moon before a man could ever rest in peace at Star B.

Comstock looked down the wide valley. It was worth losing rest and sleep for. Peace came to those who fought for it.

"We're getting one devil of a collection of guns," Sky Joe said. "Maybe we can go in the hardware business, instead of raising hogs."

There were four men at Star B now. The house was in one place, and they were in four other places all night long.

And nothing happened.

"Bad steer?" Comstock asked Sky Joe at breakfast.

Sky Joe was gaunt and tired from lack of sleep. He shook his head. "Something changed, that's all."

"What was supposed to happen?" Button asked, with his mouth full of pancakes.

"Maybe Burden George was dropping in," Comstock said. "Maybe anything . . . who knows?"

"You really sent in by the governor?" Buck asked.

"I didn't say so."

The two lads looked at each other. They were convinced that the rumor was true. Lack of denial cinched it with them. Comstock began to get an idea. It was a dangerous one, but just staying in the country was dangerous.

CHAPTER
FIVE

Until late afternoon they took turns at sleeping. It might be that way for a long time, Comstock thought. They needed a bigger crew, and they ought to carry the action away from Star B. On top of that, there was the business of restocking the ranch. He had bitten into the biggest chunk of his whole life, but he would chew it, or chew lead.

"Carry the war to them?" Sky Joe blinked. "With what?"

"My guess is we'll be let alone for a while. That's when we want to make our play. We got to have a crew. I figure we can get some of it the way we got Button. I can get Lamb, for one, I think. Maybe, when the word spreads to some of the small ranchers that have been cleaned out, they'll rally in here."

Sky Joe was dubious. "I dunno. But it's sure worth trying." He put a long foot on the corral fence and glanced at the house, where Button and Buck were sleeping. "Them two, I think, will be all right. I hope."

"Does Lamb ever stay around his ranch?"

"Yeah. Whenever he can. He's got a right pretty wife."

Comstock grunted. "That's news to me." Lamb had not mentioned that on the ride north of Buffalo. Come to think of it, Marty had not mentioned much about anything.

"Tell me one ranch that's still in business, and yet not swinging with Pistol in the land grabbing."

"Triangle K. Sam Crouse is so hard-headed and honest, it's plumb painful. Next to Star B, Triangle K is the spread that Collins wants worst."

Comstock kept a watchful eye on the ridges. "This Crouse would back a meeting of small ranchers, wouldn't he?"

"Meetings. Hell, we had a hundred meetings."

"But never with the governor's investigator."

Sky Joe stared long and hard. "Then you know . . . ?"

"Nothing at all about it. You don't have to say I'm the man. Don't even hint it. Deny it, and everybody will believe what they want to believe."

"That'll work, that part, all right. But what's the good of a meeting?"

"We won't lick the whole country by ourselves."

"So far we've done fair."

"Just so far, Sky Joe. You ride west, and I'll ride east. We'll both try to hire hands. Tell every little rancher about the meeting at Triangle K tomorrow night."

Sky Joe thinned his lips and shook his head. "One thing about you . . . you sure don't wait for something to happen."

"Waiting will ruin us."

"Yeah." Sky Joe squinted at the west ridge. "Suppose we can recruit a big crew. You got money enough to pay 'em? There's taxes coming up on the place, too. We got to have supplies. We got to have horses, other things."

"How much will that run?"

Sky Joe named a figure.

"That'll just about clean me."

"How about the cattle we need?"

Comstock made an impatient gesture. "One bridge at a time, Sky Joe. If a man stopped to figure everything that might go wrong, it would scare him so bad he wouldn't have time to do anything but die of the worrying collywobbles. Now, tell me how to find the small ranches."

By the time the cutbanks were gathering dusk, Comstock had visited three small ranches. One was deserted. At the other two he was dubious of the sticking qualities of the men he talked to, and made no offer to hire them. He told them about the meeting at Triangle K. They did not commit themselves about attending.

This was a scared range where too many had been afraid to commit themselves. He rode on to the 78, Lamb's place.

It was in a valley bottom, on good water. A windbreak of small cottonwoods was sprouting all around the ranch site. There was no house or other buildings. Smoke was still coming from where they had been.

So this was where Pistol had switched its play last night.

Comstock rode toward a tarpaulin shelter. Under it a woman was kneeling beside a stocky man who lay on blankets. Outside, two men were squatted near their horses. One came up like a steel spring when Comstock rode into view.

That was Manny Fields. The one who did not rise was Burden George.

"Push on the lines, Manny, and you won't be worth burying," George said quietly. "Swing down, Comstock."

Comstock hesitated. While his weight was in one stirrup, he wouldn't have a show. He made a flashing new assessment of the gray-haired man, remembering several little things about him.

He got down without hurry, and it made a long, tight moment before both feet were on the ground.

Manny Fields had murder in his dark face. George was watching him, looking up past heavy, gray brows. The rustler boss stood up with litheness almost incredible in one so large. "Little man," he said to Fields, "if you're set on it, go out of gunshot hearing with him." He inclined his head toward the scene behind him.

"There's lots of time," Fields said.

It was Marty Lamb on the blankets. His face was pinched hard against the bones, and his breathing spoke of death. The woman tried to give him water, and he shook his head feebly.

"Pistol," George said. "Last night. You wonder why so many men took to rustling?"

With his hat in his hands Comstock knelt beside the dying man. The woman looked at him and did not see him.

50

"Marty, it's me . . . Jim."

Lamb's smile was a death mask grimace that would ride lonely nights of memory. "Jimmy Cornstarch," he whispered, and the nickname rolled away the years clear back to boyhood on the Gunnison. "I'm sorry, Jim. I got you in a mess."

"It's all right, Marty. It's all right."

Lamb closed his eyes. The hand that held his wife's tightened a little. Comstock looked at the woman. She did not say it, but she wanted him to leave.

He went outside, boiling with savage anger against the whole situation that had brought about this thing. Fields's white-toothed grimace became a focal point.

"How's the stomach, Manny?" Comstock asked.

The little gunman read Comstock's tone, and weighed his chances — and then turned away. He walked slowly to his horse, preserving some face with his leisurely retreat. He expended fury by roweling the horse brutally as he plunged away into the growing gloom.

"I guess you know . . . don't ever make no mistake with Manny," George said.

"Good advice. It goes for the rest of your crew, too, I suppose."

"Don't bite at me, Comstock. I once owned a good layout here . . . before things like this began to happen."

Anger was clawing Comstock. "I still owe you something for the deal the other night, George. Would you like to collect the other way . . . ?"

"Are you talking about owing me for keeping Fields and Sioux from gunning you on the ground after Utah Slim laid you out . . . or for letting you get clear as easy as I could?"

Comstock considered several items about George, the man's cool way, his apparent sincerity in regretting Comstock's premature attempt to leave the rustler roundup camp, and his unmistakable contempt for Fields. It came to Comstock that no matter who Burden George sided on this gunsmoke range, the man was built solidly all the way through.

"All right, George. Thanks."

"None needed."

They stood silently in the gloom, with the breathing of the dying man behind them pawing at Comstock's nerves. Mrs. Lamb was talking softly, as if to a fretful child.

"You're sure this was Pistol?" Comstock asked.

George tipped his head toward the shelter. "She saw Anse Welch when they shot down Marty. Anse is Collins's foreman."

After a long silence Comstock said: "George, will you throw in with me and Sky Joe at Star B?"

The gray head wagged slowly.

"You'll lose in the end."

"Maybe," George said.

It was too bad, Comstock thought. He had not met a man who he would have liked for his side better than Burden George.

They built a fire, so that Mrs. Lamb could see, and then they hunkered down in the shadows beyond the flames — and waited without speaking until Lamb died two hours later.

His wife came out to the fire. She stood there staring at the flames, rubbing her hands around each other, her face blank. She might be a pretty woman, Comstock thought, but right now it gave him an odd, scared feeling to look at her.

George went over to her. "Let's see, Kate, you were married just about three months ago, just before Marty lost the last of that mortgaged herd to Pistol, wasn't it?"

That was a devil of a thing to say, Comstock thought.

"Three months ago last night." Mrs. Lamb might have been talking in her sleep.

"Remember the first night he brought you to a dance, at the Triangle K?"

"I remember," Mrs. Lamb said tonelessly.

George went on talking, plunging back into her life with ruthless insistence. Little by little expression came back to her face. It seemed to Comstock that she relived her married life as George talked on and on, right up to the night before. And then it seemed to Comstock that she stiffened and started to resume her blank look of shock.

"I liked that boy, Kate. I was sorry to see him killed." George said his next words like a preacher. "He was a good, faithful husband, Kate."

Mrs. Lamb broke then and began to cry. George put his arms around her. Sweat gleamed on George's face as he glanced into the dark where Comstock squatted, and made a tiny twisting motion with his head, as if to say: "Man, that was rough."

A little later, with the woman still sobbing, George said softly: "Comstock."

Comstock had heard it, a horse coming harder than a horse should move at night, even on these open, rolling hills. He made a wide circle in the darkness and came between the sounds and the fire. Just one man out there.

And that made the second time he had mistaken Caroline Collins for a man. He put his gun away when she hailed the fire. She did not know he was there as he moved behind her when she went toward George and Mrs. Lamb.

"I just found out," Caroline said.

Of course there would be a lot of silence at Pistol about the burning and killing, Comstock thought. Watching from beyond the firelight, he observed that Caroline and George accepted each other's presence without question. They might even be friendly, Comstock thought.

Caroline took over the job of comforting Mrs. Lamb. They, too, seemed to be friends. More than ever it struck Comstock that this was not the usual rangeland war, nonetheless deadly, but a complicated tangle with ties crossing from side to side.

"Comstock has been telling the small ranchers to meet tomorrow night at Triangle K," Caroline said.

"*Hmm.*" George nodded at some thought of his own. "Come in, Comstock."

Caroline jerked her head around when she heard Comstock's boots behind her. Surprise ran across her face, and then she was studying him carefully.

54

"I guess you two know each other," George said.

"Yeah. We were pretty close to each other one night."

"Make yourself clear, Comstock." George's pale eyes were deadly cold, and his voice was bleak.

"You misunderstood me," Comstock said. "I was not . . ."

"Pick your words more carefully, then."

Looking at Burden George, thinking of the terrible controlled power there was in the man, Comstock remembered that Sky Joe had said Caroline was safe anywhere she wanted to ride on this range. It had always been Comstock's personal knowledge that he feared no man — but right now he knew he was just a little afraid of George, and was not shamed by the fact.

"Burden . . . I mean Puritan," Caroline said, "Mister Comstock meant he grabbed me in the dark the night before last when he thought I was a man prowling the Star B Ranch."

"Let him say that, then."

"I apologize to Miss Collins. Now don't push any farther, George." Comstock's anger was forming, and that removed any fear of the rustler chief.

George gave him a long stare. The brittle look faded from the pale eyes. "I'm a touchy man about some things, Comstock. I see I took you wrong."

Mrs. Lamb was not crying in Caroline's arms now. She was watching and listening, completely back in the world once more.

"Kate, would it be all right if I took you over to the Triangle K? I know Sadie Crouse would . . ."

"No." Mrs. Lamb shook her head. "Sam Crouse was a bitter enemy of Marty's, after Marty went out with . . . with . . ." She looked at George and was silent.

George nodded. "No, Caroline, Triangle K won't do." He moved away from the fire. "Where shall we bury Marty, Kate?"

"Right here . . . on his land," the woman said calmly. "And I'll stay . . ."

"You can't," Caroline said. She looked at Comstock, as if for help.

Comstock had no help. All he could think of was Pistol, and he knew Mrs. Lamb would never go there, and so did Caroline. He started away to help George.

"Mister Comstock," Mrs. Lamb said. "You were Marty's friend. You talked him into quitting the rustlers. Now . . ."

"He quit the bunch?"

"The day after you did. Those men last night wouldn't believe him when he said so. Anse Welch . . ." Mrs. Lamb looked at Caroline, whose face showed the strain of her position. "Mister Comstock, I hear that you are running Star B. You and Sky Joe will need a cook. I've got to stay in this country and fight to hang on to everything Marty and me own."

A woman cook at Star B? A pretty woman? That would be trouble within trouble.

"Star B is marked for killing," Comstock said. "That's a dangerous place for a woman. Anytime, we expect . . ."

"What was it here last night, Mister Comstock?"

"Well, I . . ." Caroline was looking at him with an expression that said he ought to do it. That irritated him. Two women against one man with big trouble of his own, and Caroline a beautiful woman with the firelight running on her dusky skin. If she said anything, he could fight back with a man's right to make the decisions. But Caroline only looked at him, and let him make his decision, as he had done with Button.

It was not fair. Mrs. Lamb, with her tear-marked face, her husband dead under the canvas shelter, speaking of holding onto land, speaking of Marty's friendship for Comstock.

In the end it was the fact that Mrs. Lamb was a fighter who wanted to hold on that weighed the most with Comstock.

"Well . . . Sky Joe, maybe he . . ."

"I'll take care of Sky Joe," Caroline said. "And I will send someone over from Pistol to make the whole thing work out for Kate and everyone else."

"All right," Comstock said. *All men are born damned fools*, he told himself.

From the darkness George called: "Somewhere here on the south hill, Kate?"

"Yes. There where it will overlook the valley." She rubbed her cheeks. "Thank you, Mister Comstock." Mrs. Lamb went into the darkness.

Comstock looked questioningly at Caroline.

"She's all right," Caroline said. "She just wants to walk out there alone for a while."

Comstock looked at the long, clean lines of the woman at the fire. There was nothing of her father in her, except the coloring of her features. It struck him that here was a woman fitted to this country, a beautiful woman. Perhaps in days to come, when a man could ride the grass without constant attention to his back trail . . . A lot of men up here must have looked at Caroline Collins with the same thoughts Comstock had.

The sound of a shovel came from the hill. Comstock started in that direction.

"Mister Comstock."

He went back to the fire. He would come back anytime Caroline Collins made such music of his name, and that was not weakness, either, any more than his healthy fear of Burden George.

"I'm sorry I gave you so much trouble the other night," Caroline said. "I thought it must be a friend of Sky Joe's after I saw the buckskin, but when you grabbed me . . ."

"Neither of us could help it." Comstock hesitated. "I can understand your friendship with the Lambs, and others like them, but Burden George . . ."

"Is he a rustler, against both small and large ranchers, with only Pistol being really large any more. Up here a man is not completely responsible for what he does sometimes. Before George started on his own, he was foreman of Pistol. He taught me to ride and use a gun. His wife was the only mother I ever knew."

Comstock looked from her face to the flames. He understood, but the thought persisted that she had warned George of the meeting. Still, he would have known anyway, and, as Sky Joe had said, there had been many meetings of the same kind.

"Were you sent up from Cheyenne?"

Comstock shook his head. "Was George?"

"He lives here."

"Still, it could be . . ."

"Don't even suggest it. His men, or someone from another rustler crew, would kill him from the dark on the strength of a rumor like that."

"Like your father wanted to hang me on the strength of the same rumor?"

She nodded bleakly. "I intended to try to save you, but I doubt that I would have had courage to use my gun if my father called my hand. He would have, too."

"I think you would have made a good try." Comstock was pleased, and some of his thoughts ran through his expression.

"Not because of you, Mister Comstock, and particularly not your face. Only because I'm deathly sick of what my father has been doing for years."

"You're not alone. Will you name me men I might be able to hire to help me and Sky Joe?"

She gave him six names, and told him where he might find the men. And then she named three more — Pistol riders.

They stood there silently for a while. The sounds of the busy shovel came from the hill where George was digging in the dark. Over near the burned house Mrs. Lamb was sobbing again.

"You'd better leave. You have a long ride to make," Caroline said. "I'll take Missus Lamb to Star B tomorrow."

Comstock looked toward the shelter. "I want to stay until . . ."

"Marty would understand," she said. "Marty was a little light for this country, in a way an odd sort of friend for a man like you to have, but he would understand. You'd better do what you have to do, Mister Comstock."

He got on his horse, and, before he turned it east, he sat a moment looking at the tall woman at the fire. Even at a distance he thought he could see what he had seen close up, how much this tangled, dirty mess was costing her. Rustlers he could understand. They would always be a problem. Major Collins — he should have been killed years ago.

Comstock rode away.

CHAPTER
SIX

By daylight he had visited three more ranches. At the second one a rifle blasted from a window and the shot narrowly missed him, just as he was opening his mouth to hail. Tempers were being prodded by uncertainty. Three of the men Caroline had named were at that second ranch. Two of them promised to come over to Star B in a day or two. The third said he would go right now.

Comstock sent him to call upon other small ranchers.

At the other two spreads he managed to get a shaky sort of promise from one man. That was part of the country, too. A good many were waiting to see which way to jump.

He was saddle weary when he rode into the Triangle K. The long lush valley, fed by a dozen small streams coming down to a main creek, told him why Collins coveted this place. The buildings were set where rocks and timber formed a little basin apart from the valley. He saw only Triangle K four-year-olds in the valley, but not as many as there should have been on grass like this.

Two cowboys came from the bunkhouse and walked to the corners of the building, then lounged against the logs, watchful.

A brisk little man with lather on his face and a razor in his hand came down the steps of the ranch house. His gun belt was on. His underwear was rolled elbow-high, revealing the sharp contrast of white skin and brown, hard wrists and hands.

"Mister Crouse?"

"That's right." There was neither friendliness nor hostility in the little man's voice. His eyes were keen, probing points. The razor flashed in the morning sun as he resumed his shaving.

"I'm Jim Comstock. I've taken advantage of your name, Mister Crouse, by telling ranchers that there will be a meeting here tonight."

"I heard." The razor scraped down a lean cheek. The eyes stayed on Comstock.

"I thought there wasn't time to do it right, and from what I've heard of you . . ."

"Who told you?"

"Sky Joe."

"Chandler went back to the Star B, eh?"

It was the first time Comstock had heard Sky Joe's last name. He nodded. "We aim to fight."

"High time." Crouse seemed more on the friendly side now, but he went right on shaving, and he did not ask Comstock to get down. Over at the bunkhouse corner the two men rolled smokes, and watched.

"Asking a little late, will it be all right for the ranchers to meet here?"

"Cowmen are always welcome to meet at the K." The way he said it excluded Comstock.

"I'm a cowman . . . in a way."

The razor went on scraping. "I don't know, Comstock. I don't know that at all."

"You'll have to take my word."

"I don't take anybody's word. From what I hear, you seem to be sided up right, but I don't know you from Adam, mister."

"All right, you don't. Do you mind if I come to the meeting tonight?"

"Not if it's a scheme to hire my hands away."

"A man doesn't hire men away from a ranch . . . if it's a run by a white man."

Crouse's eyes were muzzle-steady points of brown. He whipped lather off the razor. "Light down, Comstock. I'll have the cook rustle you up a bait of grub."

After breakfast, Crouse suggested that Comstock stay at the Triangle K and get some sleep. "I'll take care of the one or two ranches you couldn't get to and back before dark."

"I'm obliged."

"We try to help ourselves up here," Crouse said.

There was a tough cable of resolution in the Triangle K owner, Comstock thought. No man who was not hard-gutted could have survived and held his ranch if it had been otherwise.

"You the man who was supposed to come up from Cheyenne, the last two, three years?"

Comstock shook his head.

Crouse considered some private thought. "See you tonight." He went out of the yard at a trot.

Comstock went over to the bunkhouse, where he slept until late afternoon. When he woke up, he lay in the bunk for a while, thinking that Triangle K, and perhaps Pistol, must be the only two ranches in all the country where a man could sleep with a reasonable assurance of security. Considering the reservoirs of hate Pistol had stored against itself, there was sure to be a day when its people would not rest easily. Caroline Collins ought to be away from Pistol when that time came.

Still thinking of Caroline, Comstock got up and shaved with a razor he borrowed from one of the cowboys who seemed to have no other duty than being a guard at the ranch.

"What's this Association I've been hearing about?" Comstock asked.

"Ranchers' organization. It used to do a little good, before Major Collins busted it up by trying to run everything."

"Uhn-huh." Comstock's thoughts slipped from Collins to his daughter.

"You the governor's man?"

"Now whatever gave you that idea?"

The cowboy grunted. He was satisfied in his own mind. "Nothing. Nothing at all," he said.

Just before sunset Crouse came back with Sky Joe. The latter had gone west from the Star B, then ridden a big circle to the south and had met Crouse at the Five Bar A.

64

"There'll be a few here, anyway," Sky Joe said. "I heard what happened to Lamb."

Crouse spoke slowly. "Welch and the Pistol riders probably didn't know it was true Lamb had quit George. Still, they should have held off. They made things worse all around."

"That's what Collins wants," Comstock said. "The worse it is, the more chance he has to grab what he wants. When he's got his hooks into the land, he can turn on the rustlers."

"A few of us have always known that," Crouse said.

"What makes Pistol so tough?" Comstock asked.

"Size. Money. A crew of eighty men. All that, and the fact that Collins is bold and smart."

"Plenty of gun hands?"

Crouse shook his head. "I said he was smart. Gunmen pile up more trouble than they're worth. No, Collins . . ."

"Speak of the devil," Sky Joe said.

A red-gold stallion with a rider in cavalryman's posture was coming up the valley. Comstock wondered if Collins ever arrived anywhere except at a gallop.

They waited, and Collins came into the yard and up to them. He ignored Sky Joe and Comstock. "My daughter here, Sam?"

Crouse shook his head.

Caroline probably had stayed last night with Mrs. Lamb and George at the ruined 78. Right now she should be on her way home, after leaving Mrs. Lamb at Star B. Let Collins sweat, Comstock thought, unless he asked.

If Collins was worried, he hid it well. "The Association is meeting tonight, eh?"

"Not the Association, Collins," Crouse said. "Just some men."

The Pistol owner started to swing down. "I suppose we'll chew over the rustler problem again, and . . ."

"Not *we,*" Crouse said. "Stay up, Collins. You're not invited."

"What's that, Sam?" Collins seemed genuinely surprised, and injured. But a tightness had already built around his eyes before he looked at the Star B owners. "These two been feeding you . . . ?"

"No," Crouse said. "You and me have known a long time where we stood. Because of Caroline, I haven't spoken up the way I should have. Now you've heard me, Collins. Ride out."

There was a hard, tight moment. Then Collins said: "Well, by God, Sam!" He whirled the stallion and went out of the yard.

It was too simple. The three in the yard looked at each other, sharing uneasiness.

"He's smart," Sky Joe said. "Worries me. Always did."

Counting Sky Joe, Comstock, and Crouse, there were sixteen ranchers in the long main room of the Triangle K. Hard-handed men in worn boots. Two overhead lamps put patches of light on wind-burned faces, and showed the doubt and hope in eyes that kept going back to Comstock. He was thinking that down in Colorado sixteen ranchers representing what these men did would be a powerful, established force. Break Pistol, snap the backs of crews like George's — and these men would be what they rightfully should be. It was mainly up to them, if he could make them see it.

As much as he disliked trickery, he had to continue to use it. "I'm not from the governor, and never claimed to be, but, if I was, I think I know what he would have me say." The qualification of denial worked like a charm. Around the room men looked knowingly at each other. "He'd say it was like the grass wars, a local matter to be handled by those involved. If you can't lick the country and the two-legged predators in it, you'd better go to another country. It's dragged along to the point right now where you got to fight quick and hard, or admit you're licked.

"I had an idea of making Star B a stronghold for everybody to light from. That was wrong. We want men there, and, if anybody wants to come over and go on the payroll, that's fine. Before the meeting two men said to me, why don't we scrape up every cent we can and hire an army of gunmen? The governor wouldn't like that, I'll bet. A man who hires out to fight fights only for his wages. Gunmen would bring blood and bitterness forever, no matter who won. That's no good, just like my idea of rallying a big force to Star B was no good.

"It's a personal matter for every honest man who owns a ranch. The thing to do is go back to your ranches and run 'em. Let every longrider, and those who are trying to squeeze you out, see that you aim to stay on that land and hold it. You've been scared. You've

67

been on the run. Stand hard and fast, and, believe me, that alone will create a feeling and make a change so that every crook on the grass will begin to wonder . . . 'What's happening around here, anyway?' "

"You talking . . . or the governor?" someone asked.

"Just me, Jim Comstock."

Another asked: "Who buries the dead that stood hard and fast?"

"There'll be that, yes," Comstock said. "There's sixteen of us here, maybe more that couldn't make it, or were afraid to but will later. Trouble hits one of us. There's sixteen of us, at least, to make it rough on them that caused the trouble. We do that a few times, and things begin to improve."

"As long as the sixteen last," a bearded man said.

"I heard of a man who was afraid of dying with his boots on," Comstock said. "So he went to bed and it worked fine. One day the house caught fire. He dressed and started to run outside, and a beam fell down and killed him right in the doorway . . . with his boots on."

They mulled it over, some grinning, a few laughing quietly. The bearded man said: "I ain't afraid. I'm just figuring chances."

"That's about all," Comstock said. "I've said it as a man who figures to live in the country, and not as a representative of anyone else. You've got an Association already. Maybe there's a man or two you'd like to drop. Me and Sky Joe would like to become members. That's about all the organization you need, I'd say."

As a newcomer, Comstock knew he could not have got away with outright telling them what to do, but, by the left-hand pretense of being the governor's investigator, he had got away with it.

For three hours the meeting went into ways and means. It was raining steadily when discussion ended. It seemed to Comstock that the men who rode by twos and threes into the rain were thoughtful and determined. He considered it a good sign that no one took Crouse's invitation to spend the night at the Triangle K.

Sky Joe and Comstock had three new hands when they were ready to go. Clayt Rogers was the man Comstock had hired at the ranch where he was fired on the night before. Johnny Winters was one of the two who had been at the same ranch and undecided. Now he was ready. The third, Fred Custis, was one of the men Caroline had named, a rider from a ranch far to the east. All three had come with their employers to the meeting, and had waited in the bunkhouse until it was over.

Before he took them on, Comstock talked to their bosses. Fred Custis's employer summed it up for all. "We hate to lose anybody, but we ain't been able to pay 'em for months, and maybe you're going to need men worse right now than we will."

Sky Joe said: "I'm a little worried about leaving Buck and Button alone. Let's get moving."

"Go ahead with the boys," Comstock said. "I'm going down to Pistol."

"Huh?"

"I found out that two of the men Caroline said I could hire ought to be at the ranch sometime tomorrow morning . . . this morning, now. They were driving bronc's to Pistol last night."

"I'll just go along," Sky Joe said. "Custis and the others can find the Star B."

Crouse came down from the porch into the rainy yard. "If you boys need supplies, I can spare some. It may be a while before you get a chance to send a wagon south."

"Obliged," Sky Joe said. "We ain't even got a wagon. Maybe you'll let Custis and the other two haul some over now on their horses."

"Glad to." Crouse glanced toward the house. "If Caroline's there with Kate Lamb, send word back, will you? Sadie's sorta worried."

"We'll do it," Comstock said.

"Tell Kate she's welcome here, if she'll come."

"She won't," Sky Joe said.

Crouse sighed. "I guess not. Tell her anyway. Good night, boys."

He tramped back through the mud, and made only a little shadow going through the door. A good man for the country, Comstock thought. A fighter. A sticker. Marty Lamb had wanted to stick, too. He'd planted cottonwoods around the 78, and maybe envisioned them someday breaking the wind for grandchildren.

"That was really an old gag you told about the fellow with his boots on," Sky Joe said. "Let's go to Pistol."

Pistol sat on the land with something about it that reminded Comstock of the arrogance with which Collins rode the land, his or that of anyone else. The corrals were five deep. The house was a big U, squatted on the hill, the lower story stone, the upper part peeled logs. The cook shack and the bunkhouse sat 100 yards away, lower on the hill.

The Pistol mark was on every door, and over the wheel gate on a huge burned sign.

"Leave the gate open," Comstock said.

"A good idea," Sky Joe murmured. He laughed to himself.

They rode into the yard and got down.

"Anse Welch," Sky Joe muttered. "He'd be out on the roundup, if he wasn't so busy burning ranches."

Welch came down the stone steps of the bunkhouse with an expression that said he resented the open gate and their getting down without invitation. He was a lean brown column with saddle-sprung legs. Time had rutted his face as water cuts an overgrazed range.

Comstock sized him up quickly: loyalty to hell and gone, no matter who got hurt. Like the doors, he should have the Pistol brand burned on him somewhere. He looked at the gate and at his visitors.

"You fellows raised around a Blackfoot campfire, was you?" The ramrod's voice was a shovel sliding hard on gritty boards.

"Speaking of fire, Anse . . ."

"Never mind, Sky Joe," Comstock said. "Mind if I talk to Hoya Parsons and Chapo Williams, Welch?"

"What for?"

"I'll tell them."

"What?"

"They branded . . . like cattle, Welch?"

"I ain't . . . not yet." The bald-headed man who spoke came halfway through the bunkhouse door before he stepped back to get a hat. He rolled down the steps, a chesty man, square-faced, with gray stubble on his jaws. "Who wants to talk to Hoya Parsons? Hi, Sky Joe, heard you pulled the picket pin."

"Yep." Sky Joe spat and looked at four men coming from the horse corral. One of them was Bundy, the rider who had taken a rope from his saddle to hang Comstock.

"This here's Jim Comstock, Hoya," Sky Joe said.

"*Aw!*" Parsons rolled past Welch and came close.

"Thought you might want to work for Star B," Comstock said. "No pay, no grub, but you meet lots of nice people."

Parsons had a mighty laugh. He looked sidewise at Anse Welch afterward.

"You come right in here and asked, didn't you?"

"We play on top of the table," Comstock said. He looked fully at Welch. Loyalty is fine, but it sometimes hampers action. Fury was running on the foreman's face, but he did not know his play, and, when he looked instinctively to the house for a cue, there was no one moving there but a cook who came outside one of the wings to empty a pan of water.

"Chapo! Chapo! You lazy son, get out of the bunk!" Parsons's voice rolled out, and in a moment a red-headed youth, still in his underwear, just jamming a hat on his head, peered from the bunkhouse door. He caught the tension of the yard and came out a few moments later, buttoning clothing.

72

"This here's that wild man, Comstock," Parsons said. "He wants to hire up. No pay, no nothing, but a chance to get shot in the back!" Parsons laughed again.

The four came up from the horse corral and stopped behind Welch, whose face was a furrowed gray mask.

Chapo buckled his belt. "Before breakfast, Hoya?"

"You'll be fat like me, if you keep thinking about your gut all the time," Hoya said. He looked at Welch. "You know something, Ansey, for a long time I been figuring you could spare me and Chapo. I guess maybe we'll just get our pay and kiss you a fond good bye."

"Let Chapo talk for himself." The foreman's thin lips barely moved.

"Yeah, Hoya, you and your big mouth." Chapo buttoned his shirt. "After a heap of thought, I've decided to go. You got any grub at Star B?"

"Don't ever come slinking back, when Star's just another piece of range," Welch said. "You'll get what's due you on the payroll when Mister Collins comes back."

"Now," Hoya said. He was no longer a clown, but a hard, gray-whiskered oldster. "You can count, Ansey."

"Get your pay from Mister Collins . . . later."

"Now." Hoya made a slow move with his right hand and pushed Chapo farther aside.

"These men are ready to leave," Welch said to the four behind him. "See that they close the gate."

It was Hoya's play, so Comstock did not speak. He and Sky Joe watched the four at the ramrod's back.

Bundy broke the thing before it started. "The other day I almost put a rope around a man's neck, without

thinking the thing out. I might've done it. I thought I
had enough of Pistol then, but when a spread says
no pay because a man quits when they don't want
him to . . . I know I got enough. Want another hand,
Comstock?"

"It's up to Hoya now. He's Star B's foreman."

Under his breath Sky Joe said: "*Whew*. Fifty percent
of the time . . ."

"Come along, Bundy," Hoya said. "You'll do."

"One thing I forgot. If any of you three was at the
Seventy-Eight night before last . . ." Comstock shook
his head.

"None of us," Hoya said. "Anse is the fire stick and
the widow-maker," he added wickedly, and waited.

Welch did not break. Comstock watched that
individual give way before consideration of what was
best for Pistol. Blood here in the yard was not the best,
as Welch saw it. He was unafraid, but he had been
foreman too long and not one who made all major
decisions himself. Welch did not wilt. He played it safe.
"Come get your money," he said.

Cantering up the valley, Parsons let his huge laugh go.
"I feel like a man that's been forking out stables for a
long time and finally went to a barbershop and got all
cleaned up!"

Comstock looked back. Anse Welch was walking
slowly across the yard to close the gate.

CHAPTER
SEVEN

They came over the east ridge and should have raised the Star B. There was no Star B. Even the grass in the yard had burned to the soil.

Comstock was thinking of Caroline when he broke the buckskin ahead with a startled lunge.

The three men they had sent on ahead from the Triangle K the night before came from the timber at different points. Custis was holding a double-bitted axe that glinted as he grounded it. Button limped out, and, behind him, Caroline and Mrs. Lamb.

"In the middle of the morning the day after you left," Button explained. "We saw 'em coming. We forted up with all the guns, behind some logs we'd cut back in the timber, like you and Sky Joe said to do. They couldn't get us out of there, but some of 'em sneaked in with the house between them and us and set it afire. They rode away. I told Buck to wait, but he went down to put out the dry grass burning toward the corrals. Manny Fields was hiding in front of the house. He gunned Buck without a chance . . . and just kept shooting after he was down. I couldn't see too good because the smoke was coming toward me. I missed my shot, and Fields got away."

"They got you in the leg?" Comstock asked.

"Just a little. Nothing much. Miss Caroline fixed it up." Button could hardly stand.

Comstock looked at the women. "You two all right?"

"Why shouldn't we be?" Caroline said. "We didn't get here until late that afternoon."

Sky Joe's long face was calm. "All of George's gang, Button?"

"Just Sioux Chambers and Fields. There was Pug Ellis, with his arm in a sling, the three that was here the other day, four from another bunch . . . some of Hiatt's men, I think."

"Uhn-huh," Hoya said. "Rastus Hiatt and the Ellis boys sometimes throw in together. Sioux and Manny were out of their territory."

"You know quite a bit about all the longriders, Hoya," Comstock said.

Parsons pushed his hat back with his wrist and swiped his shirt sleeve across the front of his bald head. Color began to rise in his face. He glanced quickly at Caroline and away. "I ought to know something about 'em. I dealt with all of 'em for Pistol. I tallied the Pistol stuff they turned back. One dollar a head."

Sky Joe's mouth was trap-tight. "Say that sort of slow, Hoya."

Hoya's face was flaming red. He hesitated.

"Go ahead," Caroline said tonelessly. "It won't embarrass me. I knew about it last year."

"Like this," Hoya said. "These rustlers down here pass their stuff on to three, four gangs that drive into Montana. About last year, the brand inspectors up north got so tough that putting big herds through was rough sledding. The Ellis boys and the rest had to cut their loop size some because they couldn't get shet of everything they could steal. They started running butcher wagons in all directions. I reckon that helped some, but there was still too many cows here for 'em to swallow. That's when Pug Ellis put through the deal with Pistol. Take Pistol stuff along with the rest, so it wouldn't look too bad, but turn it all back for one buck a head. It cost old . . . Pistol . . . to beat the band. It ruined 'most everybody else. Pretty soon the other gangs caught on. They made the same deal as Pug." Hoya spat and turned his head. "I did the tallying. Pete Ellis told me himself there was an agreement not to run the thing too far into the ground . . . or Pistol would go out full force against the rustlers." He pulled his hat low and stared at the ground. "That's how come I know plenty about every long-rope bunch here."

It fitted fine, Comstock thought. A dollar a head for cows that came home was a small price in a long-range plan to ruin every other rancher, and gain a grass empire for about ten cents an acre. God help the rustlers then!

Comstock took a long time rolling a cigarette. Everyone was watching, waiting. He lit the cigarette and peered through the smoke at three sticks of felled timber. "Your idea, Custis?"

Custis turned the axe in his hands. "Miss Caroline said we might as well start on a new house."

"I couldn't think of a better idea, huh, Sky Joe?"

"Just one . . . but not here at the ranch."

77

"In a minute," Comstock said. "How you fixed for grub, Custis?"

"We brought over as much as we could." Custis tallied faces. "It won't last long now."

"I think," Comstock said, "we'll go after some right soon, roundup grub in a rustler wagon. Hoya will know about where to find it."

Parsons grinned. "Man, you're talking! I've always wanted to ride in on those boys in the proper manner." His square, gray-stubbled face went grim. "Buck Skelton was a good kid."

"Miss Caroline, there's nothing more anybody can do to Star B now, but it still ain't a healthy place. I wonder if you and Missus Lamb could go to the Triangle K . . . ?"

"No," Kate Lamb said. "Not me. This boy" — she looked at Button — "can't ride with you. I'll stay here with him."

Comstock needed the man he had promised to send to Triangle K to relieve Mrs. Crouse's mind about Caroline. He mentioned the fact that Mrs. Crouse was worried, and Caroline reacted exactly as he had hoped.

"I'll go over myself," she said, "on my way to Pistol."

Comstock thanked her with a look, and he saw that she had known his thoughts all the time. He did not mind a bit.

"Well," Sky Joe said, "which way, Hoya?"

"Wait'll I pick me a nice long gun out of that there log fort of Button's," Hoya said.

★ ★ ★

The night was a dirty black blanket that let the cold strike where it would. They pulled their horses close together in high grass they could not see, and Hoya, who had led all the way, put his hands under the front edges of the saddle blanket to warm his fingers.

"You can't see the fire down there," he said, "because there ain't none. They expect you, Comstock, with maybe two, three others. The wind's against us, and Pug's got a little pinto mare that'll whinny at a week-old horse track. High willows all along the crick. You could dig a mile before finding a rock to lay behind on either ridge. They never used to bother, but tonight they likely got a guard out . . . besides the pinto mare. There's your camp . . . and what do we do?"

"We leave the horses here, and walk in for breakfast."

"It's a long walk for a fat man," Hoya said. "But breakfast is a time when a man has his mind on grub, even a rustler."

"I'd like to eat right now," Chapo said.

Sky Joe chuckled. "They say a bullet in a full belly ain't very good." He swung down into the dewy grass.

"I'd say a bullet in an empty gut wasn't so good, either." Chapo got off his horse. "This dew would drown a tomcat."

"Cinch up anything you're wearing that's going to rattle," Comstock said.

Johnny Winters expelled breath with the shaky sound of a man who is nervous and cold. "My teeth won't cinch," he said.

★　★　★

Comstock could not see a thing, but he had heard the horses, and knew the camp was right below. He lay in the deep grass and waited, with Hoya on one side and Chapo on the other.

Star B could not ride out of this if it got too hot, because the horses were a mile away, untended. Maybe farther now.

Pre-dawn was a feeling. Dawn was ragged layers of dim light, cold, wet grass, and utter quiet down where the wagon was taking shape.

Then they stirred, coming out of their blankets like an honest crew on roundup. Pug Ellis slid out from under the wagon. First he took a good look at the horses picketed below camp, and then he began to adjust the blue bandannas of his sling.

Smoke crept close to the ground before the campfire began to take hold and blaze. Humped in the saddle, careless now that the night was gone, the guard crossed from one ridge to the other and took a brief look at the open country. His horse snaked its neck and shied a little when he started toward camp. The guard must have been then between Custis and Clayt Rogers.

Looking from his tunnel in the grass, Comstock had a bad moment, remembering how quick on the trigger Rogers was. But the guard was cold and the night was gone. He jerked the horse's head around and went into camp, where he tried to warm at the fire. The cook cursed him irritably.

The pinto mare was lame as it went toward the willows. Comstock could not tell for sure, but he would have bet that a bullet gash on the left shoulder made it walk that way. Button had said that Ellis rode the pinto when his gang burned Star B.

A little later Comstock saw a mound of soil where the digging had been easy near the creek. Uhn-huh. Button and Buck had done their best. The rustlers had only a dozen men below.

Peering through his tunnel in the grass beside Comstock, Hoya said it an instant later: "Twelve. You and me and Chapo could get Pug and two others right off."

"And lose most of the rest. You wouldn't want to bust 'em that way, anyhow, would you?"

"No. I see three down there that oughta have a chance. This way's best, if it works . . . and we don't get bathed to death by dew before it's over."

The rustlers saddled up before breakfast. They were around the wagon and at the fire when Comstock rose.

"We got you dead to right, Ellis! You're surrounded!"

Standing, eating at the tailboard, Ellis drew his gun with his left hand almost before he looked up the ridge. Cold-bloodedly he judged the distance and did not fire, but someone snatched a rifle from a bedroll and sent a snap shot that clipped grass near Comstock's knees.

As he dropped, Comstock sent one shot back. It was a miss, he knew. Chapo and Hoya opened up with their rifles. A man running with a tin plate in his hand went down. He rolled under the wagon, and a moment later was firing with a six-gun.

Pug Ellis stepped behind the wagon. His shouts came up the hill. "Comstock! Three, four with him! Get around behind them! Watch that other ridge!"

Comstock took three shots at a man sprinting toward his horse. He knocked the fellow's legs from under him on the last try. Six others went up in leaps. They churned through the creek, got behind the willows, and went streaking down the valley. They were under the guns of Sky Joe, Bundy, and Johnny Winters, spread fifty yards apart on the other ridge. But the three waited, according to the plan.

Two of the rustlers went up toward them. Four went on down the valley, and then swung to come in behind Comstock.

Smoke was drifting all around the wagon wheels, where men lay with tarps and bedrolls piled in front of them. Ellis was standing at one corner of the wagon, shooting a rifle with one hand, jamming the stock in the crook of his right arm when he worked the lever. He put a shot so close to Chapo that the redhead froze before he got up nerve to raise his head again. And then the rifle lead of the others made him duck again.

Comstock and Hoya were pinned tight, too. Ellis was a good commander. He had reacted about as Comstock thought he would.

Somewhere down Comstock's ridge a man shouted triumphantly. "They ain't got any horses!"

Comstock heard about it afterward. Custis and Rogers, nearly trampled, rose up like Indians and shot two men from their saddles as they passed. Rogers got a horse with his next two shots, and the fall cracked the rider's shoulder. Rogers and Custis had to fight like trapped men on foot, with no place to run. They doubled up on the fourth man. He broke for open country, got clear, and did not stop.

On the other ridge Sky Joe killed a horse. The rider rolled through the grass, took advantage of its cover, and finally escaped to the willows. Johnny Winters, scared all the way, took his man with one rifle bullet through the chest when the rustler spun his horse to fire at Sky Joe.

That left the wagon under crossfire. In little spurts those on the ridges who had been spread widely began to close in to easy range. Sky Joe kept shooting at the horses, until Hoya groaned.

A man at the wagon broke clear, running for a plunging sorrel. Above the sounds of firing Comstock heard Pug Ellis cursing the fellow. The man rode straight down the creek, staying in it, with the willows making him a poor target. He was the second and the last that escaped.

Three times Comstock yelled for Ellis to give up. The rustler leader either did not hear, or would not listen. His men were dying. Sky Joe had scattered or killed most of the horses, and was still firing at the wounded ones.

Pug Ellis was savage courage all the way. He bullied two men into charging with him, straight up the hill on foot. He was cursing Comstock as he ran. His two companions could not take it. They turned back and dived under the wagon.

Ellis went on, the blue bandannas fluttering on his useless right arm, a six-gun out before him in the left. He did not have a chance, and he did not care.

Hoya muttered under his breath, and shot past him at the wagon. Comstock yelled at Ellis to stop and drop his gun. The man came on, with bullets from the opposite ridge slicing grass around him as Johnny Winters fired.

Chapo, perhaps angry because he had been frozen to the ground with the nerve scared out of him a while before, shot Ellis twice and dropped him dead, face down, both arms folded under him.

Down at the wagon a red bandanna came out on a rifle barrel and waved frantically. It was the wrong color but it served.

Hoya caught a horse before doing anything else. "That Sky Joe," he said, "would have a fat man walking all the time."

Custis and Rogers came off the ridge, driving before them the rustler with the broken shoulder. "This is the bunch that burned us out," Custis said. "He admitted it."

Four rustlers were left alive. One of them was dying. Hoya gave him water, put a folded blanket under his head, and rolled a smoke for him. "I wish you hadn't been in this, Ken."

The dying man grinned faintly. "So do I." He could not get tobacco smoke into his lungs. "I always said Pistol would double-cross us someday . . ."

"We ain't from . . ." Hoya let it go. It made no difference to the rustler now.

After a while they buried him with the others, burning names for headboards in pieces of boxes taken from the wagon. There were four last names that the survivors did not know.

Star B took the wagon, leaving behind only the personal gear of the gang. They left two horses for the survivors, giving no advice, making no threats.

They went down the valley and left the rustlers sitting there, with the fresh mounds to remind them of the future.

"I ain't got much stomach for it," Sky Joe said, "but it does get better results than having meetings."

"No Manny, no Sioux. Too bad they wasn't there," Hoya said.

Comstock found out about Manny Fields and Sioux Chambers when the party reached the Star B that night. Caroline was there, with a new recruit, a stout, gray-haired woman she had brought from Pistol to make it easier for Kate Lamb.

The woman was Mrs. Jamison, Hoya said later. Her husband had been range boss for Pistol, until he was killed one night two years before when Pistol was burning out a stubborn small rancher. Since then Mrs. Jamison had lived at Pistol because Caroline had taken her in, after Collins offered to give the woman enough money to reach a railroad somewhere.

Two women now, Comstock thought. *No house. No cattle, and about enough grub for a week, if Hoya went on standard rations. Just running a ranch in a peaceful, law-abiding land would be enough without . . .*

Caroline took him aside. "My father hired Manny Fields and Sioux Chambers last night."

85

Major Collins was feeling the land trembling under his feet. He was a little scared, a little desperate.

Caroline was watching Comstock steadily. He wished he knew what else she was thinking, beyond the cold fact that her father had put two killers on his trail.

"Thanks," he said. "Either one of them would be very happy to get me, anyway." He straightened his shoulders. He was dog tired from the long ride last night, sagging from the reaction after the fight this morning. "Caroline, how long can you stand it at Pistol?"

"Not much longer. For a while I thought I could slow my father down, or even stop him, but . . ."

He knew how beaten and tired she was, too, and it was worse than his physical weariness.

"Sky Joe would be tickled if you moved over here. It won't be long before there's a house. Of course, right now . . ."

"Sky Joe wanted me to come over here a long time ago. I don't know where I'll go, when I do leave Pistol."

Comstock thought of several things he wanted to say, but he only nodded. She started back to Pistol a few minutes later. Mrs. Jamison studied Comstock with the frankness of a woman who had been through the mill. She started to speak, then returned to the fire.

CHAPTER
EIGHT

Comstock took the first two hours of guard duty, and then slept like an Indian's dog the rest of the night. Hoya was talking to Mrs. Jamison and Kate when he woke a little after daylight.

"Like Kate says, my trouble was having nothing real useful to do at Pistol all the time I was there," Mrs. Jamison said. "Now I feel reborn."

Comstock heard the brisk *clattering* of utensils on the tailboard of the wagon.

"Yep. You look twenty years younger," Hoya said. "Just like a baby, almost. Can I have another pile of those wonderful pancakes before the hogs wake up?"

"Speaking of hogs . . . ," Mrs. Jamison said.

"Why, he's just a growing boy, Martha," Kate said.

"Yep." Hoya must have got the pancakes because his mouth was full of something.

Listening to the talk gave Comstock a few pleasant moments before he opened his eyes and had to look once more at burned buildings, and the long sweep of grass without a single Star B cow on it.

After breakfast he sent Fred Custis to the Triangle K to borrow tools. He sent Winters and Rogers to the ridges as lookouts. The rest of Star B went to work rebuilding.

"The old house wasn't twisted far enough to the south anyway," Sky Joe said. "I'm glad they burned it. Meant to do it myself, but never had time."

Ace, Caddo, and Slade McQuoin of Burden George's crew rode in at noon. Johnny Winters gave warning of their coming, then sent them on down after they signaled peace and talked to him briefly.

They got down when Sky Joe told them to, and came toward the wagon in silence. Ace and Caddo gave Comstock a sheepish, half-scared look. They should be worse than sheepish, Comstock thought, remembering that they had voted to have him beefed that night in George's camp.

McQuoin's round face showed little of his thoughts. He was a square-set man, with small eyes that were always in a squint, a slow-spoken man, as Comstock remembered from his two days with George. He did the talking. "We heard you needed hands."

Comstock studied the three a long time. "Where's the rest of the boys?"

"With George."

"Sioux and Manny and Utah Slim, all of them?"

"Sioux and Manny pulled out."

"Why?"

"Trouble with George."

"What kind of trouble?"

McQuoin began to roll a smoke. "They figured we ought to ride in here and wipe you out. George didn't see it that way."

"Where'd they go?"

McQuoin shook his head. He wiped the tip of a red tongue across the paper and looked at Sky Joe.

"Rustling getting too hot, Slade?" Hoya asked.

"Did Pistol get too hot for you, Hoya?"

Sky Joe made the decision. "We'll take you on, Slade. You ran your ranch, or tried to, up to three, four months back."

"About the same time Marty went out." McQuoin looked past Comstock to where Mrs. Lamb was watching. He touched his hat.

Sky Joe looked at Caddo and Ace, and shook his head.

"How long you two been in the country?" Comstock asked.

"They drifted in about six months ago," Hoya said. "They worked at Pistol until one morning they had an argument with Welch. They worked spring roundup for Sam Crouse, and, when he laid 'em off, they rode around a while, and then went out with George."

Ace and Caddo nodded together.

"You two scared out . . . or trying to be honest?" Comstock asked.

"We ain't longriders," Ace said. "We had to eat." He was a flat-cheeked man with Indian-straight hair. One side of his mouth had a tendency to droop when he was not talking. Both he and Caddo, whose oily-skinned dark face was sweating, had been friendly with Comstock during his brief stay with George. And yet they had voted for his death — or had started to.

"What do you think, Hoya?" he asked.

"All right with me."

"Sky Joe?"

"No."

"I say let's take 'em on," Comstock said.

"All right," Sky Joe said. "Your judgment's been fair so far. I said no just to balance up my fifty percent."

McQuoin worked all afternoon with part of the crew that used their horses to drag flat rocks out of the timber for a foundation. After supper he strolled down to where Sky Joe and Comstock were putting stakes in the ground to mark a corral site.

"I see you're going to be low on grub soon," McQuoin said.

"What's on your mind?" Comstock balanced the rock he had been using to drive stakes.

"Nobody but George knows we quit the gang. I think I could get your wagon through to Buffalo and back, which you can't do unless you send a half dozen men. The word is out to stop anything coming into Star B and Triangle K."

"Whose word?" Comstock asked.

"Major Collins. He sent Anse Welch over to talk to George about it."

"What did George say?" Comstock looked at Sky Joe.

"He said to hell with wrecking a supply wagon. He said his business was rustling cattle."

Anse Welch would have kept on going until he found another rustler crew willing enough for the job. McQuoin was right. It would take a strong escort to get a wagon through now, and Star B could not spare the men. Comstock thought of something else. He called Hoya over and told him to take two men and ride toward the Triangle K.

"Custis ought to be on his way back with the tools we sent for. I made a mistake sending him by himself."

Hoya took Bundy and Chapo Williams and rode away. "So you think you could get through with the wagon?" Comstock asked McQuoin. "What makes you think George hasn't told that you three ran out on him?"

"There was just him in camp when we quit. He won't talk to the others about it, and they'll figure we went where Sioux and Manny did, wherever that is. Pistol won't bother me because they'll think I'm still working for George, and the rustlers will think the same thing. I can get the wagon there and back."

"You want Caddo and Ace to go along?" Sky Joe asked.

"I'm enough," McQuoin said.

Comstock sucked in his cheeks. "We could get by on beef."

"You can't shoot beef out of rifles and six-guns."

"One rider could bring back ammunition," Sky Joe said. "Lots quicker than a wagon."

"I made my offer," McQuoin said. "I'll ride if you want me to."

It couldn't be that the man just wanted to get out of the country, Comstock thought. That chance was open any time. He made up his mind. "Wait till I see if anybody's got a pencil."

"Never mind," McQuoin said. "Your crew may be all right, but there's no need to spread this thing. Tell me what you want. I'll remember."

"I've got to make out a check on a Cheyenne bank."

"Never mind that, either. I'll get whatever you want, and you can make the check out later."

Sky Joe and Comstock looked at each other.

They spent fifteen minutes squatted near the burned corrals, listing the supplies they wanted. When they could not think of anything more, McQuoin repeated the list, and, if he missed anything, they did not know what it was.

McQuoin took the wagon out a half hour later. Comstock told the crew he was headed to bring back grub. Sky Joe shook his head. It was plain that he doubted they would ever see the wagon or Slade McQuoin again.

Hoya woke Comstock and Sky Joe sometime in the night. The smell of horse, man sweat, and tobacco smoke was on him as he squatted by their blankets in the dark. They heard the soft stamp of hoofs in the burned grass of the yard.

"We brought Custis in. Somebody got him in the rocks this side of Dirty Mary Springs."

"That was my fault," Comstock said bitterly.

Everybody in camp was awake. Comstock heard Mrs. Jamison and Kate talking under their tarp shelter farther back in the timber.

At sunrise they buried Fred Custis beside Buck Skelton. Afterward Comstock stood several minutes looking at the brightness spreading up the valley. The sun would come up every day forever on good green grass, no matter who died, no matter who won this war.

Hoya turned his hat slowly in his hands, and then put it on carefully. He had shaved that morning. Without gray whiskers he did not look old at all. "Fred's wife and kid live at Arrowhead . . . way over east," he said.

"Send Ace and Caddo to tell her."

"We might lose two more men."

"They'll be all right." They would if Slade McQuoin had told the truth about Burden George's silence.

Button insisted on going to Dirty Springs with Sky Joe and Comstock. He had run a bad fever for two days from the wound in his leg. He was gaunt and pale, but he could limp around. "I want to look for a horse track. It's a sorta dainty-stepping horse, short-gaited, goes about seven-fifty, and was shoed not more'n two weeks ago."

"Whose horse?" Comstock asked.

"Let me look at the tracks first."

Custis had stopped at the Dirty Springs to let his horse drink. He had been rolling a smoke when he started up the trail through the rocks. The torn paper and some of the tobacco were on the ground about fifteen feet away from where Hoya and the others had picked up the body. Two men had waited in the rocks, with their horses picketed over the hill. The empty cases were there, four .45s. One man's boots were boy-size; the other's were big, with the sloppy outlines that meant much wear.

Button limped up from where the horses had been picketed. "Manny Fields's red roan. He was the last to leave Star B the day he killed Buck, and I took a blamed good look at the tracks."

Comstock nodded. He was looking in the direction of Pistol. He considered riding down there alone, but he knew he had pushed his luck against Pistol as far as it would go. Anse Welch had orders now.

"Oh, oh!" Sky Joe was staring east.

Five riders had just broken over a ridge and were trotting toward the springs.

Button's bad leg gave way and he fell as he tried to run to his horse to get his rifle.

"Wait a minute," Sky Joe said. "That's Sam Crouse's bay gelding."

It was the Triangle K owner with four men. He came up the hill, and they did not have to tell him because his flat, gun-muzzle eyes read sign where flies were *buzzing* on the ground.

"One of the boys picked his horse up, headed east, this morning," Crouse said. "It occurred to me that I should have sent someone back with him."

"We figure this was Manny Fields and Sioux Chambers," Sky Joe said. "Collins hired them the other day."

One of the Triangle K riders came out of the rocks with a broad-bladed chisel that had been broken, a hammer with a broken handle, and an adze that had been blunted by beating it against stone.

Crouse folded his arms and looked across the land toward Pistol.

"Collins is not as smart as I thought," he said. "He's gone and wrecked himself."

Crouse was looking far ahead, and Comstock could understand his view, but he wanted action now. He was twenty years younger than the Triangle K owner, and therefore did not think he had as much time to wait for Pistol to tangle its own twine.

"I got more tools," Crouse said. "I'll send 'em over with a few of the boys. How you fixed for other things?"

"We got grub enough to get along," Comstock said.

"So I heard. That little deal on Spruance Creek the other day is putting new life into the ranchers, and it's running it up in the necks of the rustlers." He started to turn his horse. "Anything you need at the K, just let me know."

"We don't want to put a strain on you," Comstock said. "You're going to have trouble getting stuff yourself. The word is out to raid any wagons coming into Triangle K as well as Star B."

"Uhn-huh. I had a little trouble a time or two before about that, so I've made a practice of getting the bulk of my supplies when my riders came back from a drive south to the railroad. How are you going to get by?" He grinned. "Grabbing rustler wagons?"

"That worked once," Comstock said. "We sent a wagon south last night."

"How could you spare the men?"

"Just one man . . . Slade McQuoin."

"Oh?" Crouse turned his horse, and signaled his men. "Let me know if I can give you any help."

Watching the Triangle K riders going away, Comstock said to Sky Joe: "He didn't seem a bit surprised to know McQuoin was working for us."

"Considering how we got our crew and who's in it, it wouldn't surprise me if Burden George himself was waiting to be hired when we got back."

"You don't know how close to truth you might be," Comstock said, "if what's shaping up in my mind is right."

They had one full week of peace, during which they built the ranch house and started on a bunkhouse. With furniture, flooring, and a few other items, the ranch house was going to be all right, Sky Joe said. Right now, with only a mud-mortared fireplace, the house was given over to quarters for the women. Cooking and eating were still done outside.

Mrs. Jamison had her eye on Hoya, and the foreman, although a little nervous, as could be expected of a man who had survived to his age as a bachelor, did not seem to mind too much at that. Red-headed Chapo developed a habit of stuttering every time he had occasion to speak to Kate Lamb. Johnny Winters took to shaving every day, and one evening he startled everyone by washing his whole outfit in the creek. He spent three hours in a blanket around a private fire, drying his clothes.

Winters did not stutter when he talked to Kate, and he talked to her whenever he could, which made him and Chapo eye each other like strange bulldogs. One day, over nothing, they got into a fight while cutting timber. Sky Joe broke it up, and said nothing about it except to Comstock.

"Even in the middle of big wars, you got little wars of your own," Sky Joe said. "Take me, if I was making a play for Missus Jamison, which I ain't, then me and Hoya . . . I'm worried about Caroline, Comstock. She ain't been over in more'n a week. I'm afraid Collins . . . I don't know." A fear was running strong in him. "I think I'll go over to Pistol."

Comstock was worried, too. "She's all right, Sky Joe. You said yourself, what can Collins do?"

"I'm going over. They won't bother me . . . alone."

"Wait another day. She may drop by."

"I'm going to Pistol right now."

"Manny and Sioux . . ."

"On the range, yes. I'll have to take that chance, but I don't think Collins has dropped so low he'll let anything happen while I'm at Pistol. I'll be back tomorrow night, at the latest."

CHAPTER
NINE

Two riders came in the next day with news that a group of small ranchers from the sixteen who had met sometime before had banded up and caught a rustler crew at work. They had killed four of them outright, losing two men themselves. Then they had propped up the tongue of the rustler wagon and hanged four others.

"Whose outfit was it?" Comstock asked.

"Rastus Hiatt's. He was one of the worst."

"Nobody tangled with George yet?"

"Well, no. Some of us looked him over, but we've been sorta circling wide around Burden George. He'll get it, though, one of these days."

Right now the longriders must know they were beaten, Comstock thought. Their palmy days were gone. They would still always be on the fringes and troublesome, but once George was cleaned out, rustling on this range would take a long drop from the brazenness of wagons run openly.

What was Pistol doing? There lay the power. Major Collins wasn't going to sit tight and let his enemies grow strong. It occurred to Comstock that Ace and Caddo, who had encountered no trouble riding east to tell Mrs. Custis of her husband's death, might be able to sign on at Pistol, like Fields and Sioux. They might be able to find out plenty.

It was a temptation. Hoya had suggested it once. But it was also the kind of underhanded operation that Comstock detested. No, he would play it right on top of the table.

Sky Joe did not come back that night.

Comstock saddled up at dawn the next day to go after him.

Hoya's face was grim. "My first thought was we all oughta go, and then I figured maybe that was just what Collins figured."

"Me, too," Comstock said. He rode out alone.

There was a driver and three riders with the wagon he met before he was halfway to Pistol. The riders moved apart and sat their horses with wary expressions after they saw the savageness in Comstock's eyes when he caught sight of the man lying on a mattress in the wagon.

It was Sky Joe. His long face was gray and old. His eyes did not open when Comstock spoke his name.

Comstock moved out from the wagon and faced the riders.

"Who did it?"

After some thought, a lean, tight-eyed rider with deep gravings in his cheeks said slowly: "Anse Welch."

"Who are you?" Comstock asked.

"Becker." The fellow had the distant, contained expression of one who might sit for months around a fire and never say ten words.

"Pistol?"

Becker nodded.

"How'd it happen?"

Becker took his time. "Sky Joe and Collins had words. Sky Joe started to leave. Anse plugged him when he turned."

"Then Collins sent you back with him?"

"That was Sky Joe's idea, to go back to Star."

"How bad is he?"

The answer came slowly. "High in the chest. He's got a chance. Maybe."

Comstock waved the driver on ahead. Sky Joe's head moved loosely as the wheels bumped on. He groaned, but he did not open his eyes.

Becker moved up beside Comstock behind the wagon. The others followed. For the first time Comstock noticed that they all had their war bags and bedrolls with them.

"You fellows quit, did you?" he asked.

Becker's head made a little motion that said yes, and that it was nobody's business.

"Where's Miss Caroline?"

For a while Comstock thought Becker was not going to answer, and then he did. "South. At the Anchor."

"How far is that from Pistol?"

"Twelve miles, maybe."

Nobody spoke again until the cavalcade was going up the valley toward Star B.

"You boys want a job?" Comstock asked.

Becker shook his head.

100

They neared the ranch. Hoya and Chapo came spurring to meet them. Hoya looked at Sky Joe and began to curse in a low, violent tone.

Becker and his companions stayed with the wagon until it was in the yard, then Becker turned his horse, and the others followed suit.

"Why don't you want to work here?" Comstock asked.

Becker thought a while. "Pistol got big by burnings and killings. Dealing with the long-ropes. Then it was a bum outfit to work for. Star B'll get big killing rustlers, cleaning up the range. Smashing Pistol." He spat. "Same thing then, Comstock."

"Not while Sky Joe and me are running Star B."

Becker's tight eyes watched the men lifting Sky Joe, mattress and all, from the wagon. Then Becker looked and over the top log without too much trouble. But there were not enough men, even for fixed positions. He looked fully at Comstock as if seeing him for the first time as an individual.

"I'd dig rifle pits in this valley, Comstock, was I you. I rode with Collins in the war. He always said cavalry could overrun anything on foot. Last night he said . . ." Becker closed his mouth tightly. He pointed with his head down the valley.

He and his companions rode away.

The driver of the wagon let out a long sigh. "That Becker always sort of chilled me. Five years he was at Pistol, and today you pried more words out of him than I heard in those five years."

Thinking of what Becker had said about rifle pits and cavalry, Comstock said: "You didn't aim to go back to Pistol, did you?"

"No, sir! Not if this outfit would take me on. When a man like Sky Joe gets gunned without no chance, and you know that Collins ordered it . . ." Old loyalty to Pistol, and perhaps fear of Collins, stopped the man from finishing.

"How do you know Collins ordered it?"

"I don't know. It was a bum guess." The driver stared away from Comstock. "Where do you want the wagon?"

"Dump it in the crick, for all we care," Hoya said. "But get the team back in the timber to skid logs. Danged if I'm not sick of seeing honest saddle horses doing manual labor!"

Comstock stepped inside the house for a few moments. Mrs. Jamison and Kate were doing what they could for Sky Joe, who was still unconscious. Comstock watched for an uneasy space of time, and then went out to walk the land. *Rifle pits.*

Little fragments of decency were breaking away from Pistol, but Collins's crew was still six or seven times as large as Star B's. The Pistol owner was not going to wait for it to grow much larger. He was boiling high right now, as the shooting of Sky Joe proved. When Pistol came in, it would be as Becker had hinted, a massed cavalry charge to overrun Star B in a matter of minutes.

There was the horseshoe of timber, which had served well already, but that could be surrounded. Falling back into the trees would merely delay final settlement. To hell with the timber, except for the women.

When Collins brought Pistol in for a showdown fight — it would be there for him. From now on the pickets were going to stay farther out. The rest of Star B would work by night and sleep by day.

Manny Fields and Sioux wounded one of the pickets the next day, and chased another one clear into Star B. They sat their horses on a ridge out of rifle range and whooped and waved their hats.

Half dressed, Chapo ran to saddle a horse. Hoya stopped him. "You can't catch 'em, and no telling what's waiting where they'd lead you."

Comstock nodded. He looked around at his crew, and his gaze stopped on Ace. "You want to take day picket duty?"

Ace's droopy mouth tightened a little. "Me and Caddo been aiming to ask if we could." He glanced at the ridge. "Them two won't chase us none at all."

Ace played Indian with Fields two days later. He killed the little red roan and nearly got Fields before Sioux picked him up. The pair rode double and got away because Ace could not risk following them too far toward Pistol. After that the pickets were not molested.

Collins was getting ready. One of Crouse's riders came by to report that Pistol was cutting its roundup short and pulling all the riders back to the ranch.

The next day Caroline returned to Star B with three men and 500 cattle, brought from Anchor. It was her

103

own spread, Hoya said, given to her by her father in his honest days. "If he ever had any," Hoya added.

She knew about Sky Joe and did not speak of him until after she came from the house. "Missus Jamison says he'll live." She looked down the valley, standing beside Comstock. "Those are Star B cattle now, a small payment for what my father did to Sky Joe. I want no more of Pistol, Anchor . . . or anything that Pistol ever touched." Then after a while she said: "Collins ordered Welch to kill Sky Joe. Welch would have finished what he started, except for Buck Becker and some others."

Collins? Then she did not consider him her father any longer.

"Becker told you?" Comstock asked.

She nodded bleakly. She was sick inside, beaten down by the tensions of this murderous struggle she had tried so long to stop.

"Better get some rest." There were other things Comstock wanted to say, but they would have to wait.

Star B was at work again that night when Slade McQuoin brought the wagon in. He came from the west, having made a wide swing to throw off longriders who were suspicious of where he might be going. His squinted eyes were fiercely red, and his round face seemed to have lost flesh.

"There's your stuff," he said to Comstock, and went to bed without another word.

Some men would have spent the rest of the night telling of the dangers of the trip, Comstock thought.

★ ★ ★

Ace did not fire the warning shots the next day. He let the seven men come boldly in sight on the east ridge before anyone below knew they were close. Comstock, who was getting little sleep these days, went up after some study, and brought them in.

He knew Burden George and Utah Slim, who had knocked him flat with a pistol barrel, but he knew none of the others.

George scrubbed his gray mustache with a powerful hand and grinned. "Well, Comstock, now you got me in your camp. Do you want to start the voting now, or later?"

"I just want to hear you say where you really stand."

"I think you began to guess that quite a while ago."

"The governor's man, after all?"

George laughed. "No. Let's say I knew who he was, like Sam Crouse and Caroline and Slade McQuoin. We did what we could to help him get the goods on Pistol. Now he's got all the facts, but legal stuff can drag forever. Pistol's still alive. They'll be over tomorrow, from what I guess, Comstock."

"We'll be ready . . . if your boys can dig."

"They're badgers," George said, and laughed.

It was a day too beautiful for violence, but Ace came all the way in, not hurrying too much, and said that Pistol was coming.

"About eighty, I reckon," he said casually.

Comstock knew exactly how many men he had, wounded and otherwise, and he did not want to think of the number any more.

Hoya was already acting, joshing Mrs. Jamison as he directed the carrying of Sky Joe to the log fort in the timber.

Sky Joe muttered weakly: "Gimme a rifle. I'll get more'n horses this time."

Caroline would not stay back in the trees with the others.

"He'll lead it himself," Comstock said.

"I know he will." Her face was white. "But I can't pull the covers over my head and say it isn't so."

"You never did that, Caroline. You tried harder . . ." Those things Comstock would say afterward — if that time came.

They set their logs two high in the X legs that stood before their trench, which ran in a semicircle from where the corrals had been to the edge of the timber, with the loop-holed, unfinished bunkhouse as a strong point. A man could fire under the bottom log and over the top log without too much trouble. But there were not enough men, even for fixed positions.

The sun struck redly on Collins's stallion as it reared on the hill where he was having a look at the situation. Pistol came up behind him, and the hill was black.

"If he had any sense," Hoya muttered, "he'd run those cattle at us first . . . and then where would we be?"

"Ruined," Comstock said. But Collins was an old cavalry commander, and he wouldn't want anything in front of him but the enemy. So Comstock hoped, trusting his own judgment, trusting more the judgment of grim Buck Becker, who had ridden with Collins in the war. Rifle pits. Star B had expanded the idea.

Pistol flowed down the hill and massed in the valley, clearing the cattle out of their way. A high-spirited rider raced after a steer and tailed it on its back. Collins rode out angrily and sent the man back into ranks.

He must be making a little speech there, riding back and forth that way. Maybe, Comstock thought, he was telling them that Star B was an outlaw spread, a nest of longriders and crooked small ranchers that had to be cleaned out to the last man. Not too many would believe, but they would not care — or they would not have been riding with Pistol this morning.

"Stay down," Comstock said to Caroline. "Here they come."

Eighty men make a big force on horseback. The ground shook with their coming. Rebel yell and the short, hard cries of the cattle country. Collins carried a pistol high. The red-gold stallion carried him with flaring nostrils and ears laid back.

Across the grass and straight up the green valley, and it looked like nothing on earth could stop them. The charge held a beauty and a savagery all its own, and the men behind the logs would have something to remember — if they lived.

Anse Welch took thirty men toward the bunkhouse when the first blast of fire came from there. Maybe he thought the fear was in those who ran from the strong point to scatter along the trench, or maybe he was following orders, as he had always done. So he came on at an empty building while Collins led the rest to trample the barricade.

That first blast from the bunkhouse was the only one that Star B fired before Pistol hit the trap, a hellish trap that had made Comstock sick even when he knew it had to be. Out there before him were hundreds of potholes, just shovel size, dug straight down, one foot deep, with the sod lids back in place.

Pistol paid the price of arrogance. The horses went down with their necks outstretched, with their necks doubling under, with their riders flying. They staggered against each other, their hind legs broken. And then the barricade threw fire and smoke, and lead went into the struggling mass.

Half the charge came through anyway. The red-gold stallion led a dozen men that put their horses over the barricade before they could turn. Six-guns and rifles thinned that dozen, but the others spun their horses, leaped the logs again, and some of them escaped. Collins was one, but he was not running. He went back to reform his men, clear back across the potholes and down the valley.

Welch's crew wasted a lot of lead on the bunkhouse before he realized it was undefended, and before his men realized they were caught in a murderous crossfire from the curving ends of the barricade.

They suffered the worst because Welch did not know what to do. He had followed orders, and now he was caught, and he still thought he ought to take the bunkhouse.

Burden George stood up in the trench, his hat gone, his gray hair shining. One of his guns knocked Welch from the saddle as the Pistol foreman tried to rally men to go over the log walls. Welch never moved after he struck the ground. His men were already skimming back across the littered field. Some of them were unhorsed in the potholes, but most of them got away to rejoin Collins down the valley.

A few who had dogged it rose up and ran away from the tangle of the trap. Comstock roared for his men to let them go. There was a meager chance that Pistol had enough.

Still greatly outnumbering Star B, Pistol gathered in the valley. There would be only one time when Collins had enough.

George came over to Comstock. "Next time they'll boil off the ridges to roll up our flanks, or come through the timber."

"Sam Crouse is in the timber with five men." The flanks were the weak part. There had not been enough time to dig all the holes needed to protect the flanks.

Slade McQuoin walked over with his rifle.

"You might as well know now," George said. "Slade's the governor's strong right arm. When he went south with your wagon, he also had some business of his own. When he was here some of us did what we could to help him. I ran a rustler crew. We tried to separate the sheep from the goats. Slade got the stories of all the little ranchers driven to rustling. The governor has got the facts. Maybe he'll act, but it's a little late to help us right now. Sorry we had to rough you up, Comstock, but some of the boys were suspecting Marty, and I had to do what I could to protect him. Slade was the boy all the time."

Comstock nodded, his mind on other things. "I'm not too much surprised. I'd say the governor couldn't have picked a better man."

"Notice the wind?" McQuoin said. He looked at the timber, squinting.

"Yeah." Comstock chewed his lip. "For two days it's been coming from the wrong direction."

Bundy and Hoya went by with a wounded man, Caroline walking beside them. They headed for the bunkhouse. "Not inside," Caroline said. "They might get through to set it on fire."

Collins took a long time in the valley. He sent ten men behind the west ridge. Chapo went up and reported them riding a big circle to come in behind the timber.

"Crouse will slow 'em down a lot if they try to filter through," Comstock said. "But I don't think that's what they've got in mind."

Somewhere behind the barricade a man fired and killed a horse with a broken leg. After the long silence the shot made an unusually loud sound.

George walked along the line, talking to the men.

The sun bore down, and the waiting began to gnaw.

Then the sound of rifle fire started somewhere near the bend of the timber horseshoe. Collins's men split into two groups and went behind the ridges.

All at once the shooting ended.

Comstock shook his head. "Nothing much happened up there, except . . ." Collins would still prefer to fight

110

all his men as cavalry. Those ten back there had made only a weak feint, just enough, perhaps, to have let someone slip into the timber. Comstock wet his finger against the wind. It was still coming right down from the timber, not strong, but strong enough.

McQuoin thought so, too. "George can handle things here."

Comstock nodded. He and Slade McQuoin went back into the trees, stopping briefly at the log fort where Kate and Mrs. Jamison were watching Sky Joe.

"You stop 'em?" Sky Joe asked.

"So far." Comstock looked at Mrs. Jamison. "If you smell smoke . . ."

"We'll get him out of here, don't worry, won't we Kate?"

It was too quiet behind them, too deathly quiet ahead in the timber. An Indian, perhaps, could have walked silently, but Comstock and McQuoin wore high-heeled boots. They had to use their eyes and ears and do the best they could, and they did not make too much noise.

Comstock smelled the smoke, and made the error of looking to see if McQuoin had whiffed it, too. McQuoin stabbed him off to the side with the heel of his hand, pushing himself away with the same move, just as the shot crashed from the trees.

Going toward the ground, McQuoin fired the rifle. He shot again when he was on his elbows. Sioux Chambers's pock-marked face came up from behind some bushes. His eyes were staring at nothing. He dropped the gun in his hand, and then he fell.

111

Manny Fields broke from behind a tree, dodging like a rabbit. He might have gotten away, but he saw Comstock there alone, and whirled with his gun in his hand. Manny's first shot ripped across Comstock's leg and knocked him off balance. The second raked Comstock's ribs and knocked him back another step. Then Manny had stood still long enough; he had to twist away for his next shot. And that was when Comstock caught him and wiped the white streak of his snarl for good.

They got the fire out, tramping on it, kicking dirt. Comstock sat down suddenly.

"We got a little time yet," McQuoin said calmly. "I'll have to stop that leg from bleeding."

Little Sam Crouse came down through the trees, and was almost to them before they noticed. He looked at Manny and Sioux, and then he put his gun away.

"There were just two that got in. I was coming down after them. I think I'll go on down with you boys now."

Collins must have known from the shots, for he did not wait any longer. He came in from two sides, driving as George had predicted to roll up the flanks of the defense line.

Crouse and McQuoin began to run. Comstock limped after them.

"Go after 'em, boy!" Sky Joe said as Comstock passed the fort.

The backbone of it was broken when Comstock got where he could see. At the last moment, George had pulled everyone from behind the barricades. He took five men and went to the bunkhouse.

112

For the second time Pistol made a mistake about that bunkhouse. This time they thought it was unmanned. They came in on an empty trench, and, when they realized that, and were caught in the fire from the timber, George added to their confusion by opening up on those who had passed the silent bunkhouse.

Comstock saw the red-gold stallion go down the valley, riderless.

Pistol broke up then, spurring their horses toward the shortest way out.

It was not all sweet victory. Among the dead were Caddo and Ace and Johnny Winters. Chapo and others were wounded, Button wounded again.

Burden George went over to where Caroline was crying. He comforted her until Kate and Mrs. Jamison came and led her away.

"About half her grief was because it was her father," George told Comstock. "The other half was because he was what he was." He gave Comstock a long, hard look. "Comstock, God help you if you're not good to that girl."

"What makes you think she wants anything to do with me, George?"

"I know. She's talked to me." George walked away. He was not sure that any man in the world was good enough for Caroline Collins.

That, after a good many other things at Star B, was something that Comstock intended to disprove for Burden George. There was time now. The sun would come up every day in the valley of Star B.

Payroll of the Dead

CHAPTER
ONE

When Jim Bennington knew for sure that the second Sioux was staying with him on the left bank of the river, he paddled his soggy boat closer to the heavy current on his right, despite his being a poor swimmer. The Yellowstone was running tawny from rains deep in the mountains. The surface of it was making a seething sound and Bennington could feel the tremendous power of the river shuddering through his boat.

The crude craft was made of singed buffalo hides lashed to a framework of wild cherry wood. Bennington had started to pattern it along canoe lines and more by accident than design the boat had wound up tapered at both ends like the splinter of an angry cougar's eye. It rode low in the water but it rode well — when it was not six inches awash inside, as it was now from leakage of the pitch-daubed seams.

Three miles upstream Bennington had thought to stop and re-melt his supply of pitch for a fresh caulking job. He was swinging toward shore when the over-eager Sioux, painted black and red for the glory trail, rose in the willows and fired an arrow so close to Bennington's head that the feathered end whisked his neck in passing.

The Sioux had nocked a second arrow and the string was almost at his ear when Bennington caught him belly-deep with a rifle shot. The Indian's glory trail ended as he crumpled forward from the bank into the river. The boat spun with the current and was floating backward when a second warrior came leaping through the rust-brown willows. Bennington drove the Indian flat with two shots, but he knew that the rocking and pitching of the boat had made him miss.

The second warrior's rifle shot ripped the apron of elk skin around the cockpit of the boat. By then the current was spinning Bennington. He had to drop his rifle between his knees and grab the paddle as the boat crashed sidewise into the curling wildness of fast water.

When he got straightened out, Bennington looked back and saw the Sioux dragging his companion up the bank. Great store these Lakotas set by the bodies of their dead. Bennington hoped that the survivor had his belly full for one day; it depended on his mettle as an individual. But no such luck, for the Indian then got on a gray horse and started following downriver.

All the way from Sarsi country, bad cess to it, small groups of Sioux had kept Bennington jumping. For some reason the high plains were unduly astir. Bennington had hoped to save both work and trouble by sticking to the river.

Now he had a fair share of both. The mettle of the Sioux was tough; he kept coming. And the boat was getting so heavy that Bennington knew he would have to go ashore soon or sink. Leaping water swept him through a cut between bare hills. He saw the gray horse falling behind as it had to climb and then work its way across deep gullies.

Riding almost in the middle of the river, Bennington scanned the east bank for a good landing place. He did not like the looks of the wild water he would have to cross, but the thing to do was to put the river between him and the persistent Indian.

He started to turn across the stream. A sudden rush of water came up around his thighs, above the lashed crosspieces of the seat. A seam had popped and there was no time to make it over to the right bank. With a landman's distrust of water he had held himself ready to unload at any time; his cartridge bag and other items he could not afford to lose were around his neck on rawhide thongs and his Remington was between his knees.

The kayak still held together. He decided to make the west bank if he could, the near side, where a gravel bar of the color that gave the river its name came out like a long tongue. There was a wide streak of bad water between him and the slow swirling pool against the bar but that did not worry him as much as the position of the Sioux.

The bow of the boat came around stubbornly as he dug his paddle deep and leaned on it. He was taking water fast and it gave him a moment of panic. The bow came around. He began to paddle with all his might. Once across that churning leap of white water, he could jump out and drag the boat ashore.

He saw the rock too late. The boat went into it sidewise and began to tip upstream. Bennington grabbed his rifle and kicked free an instant before the terrible weight of the Yellowstone filled the boat, snapped the cherry wood longerons and the lashed frames, and wrapped the boat like a wet hide around the rock.

Bennington went under when he struck the water. The current twisted him in a helpless sprawl. He hit himself in the chest with the butt plate of the rifle as he flailed his arms in a wild swimming motion. He came up. His legs struck a submerged rock and the tawny waters knocked him under again.

Still clinging hard to the rifle, he dog-paddled with both hands. It was partly the swing of the current and partly his own efforts that carried him out of the heavy surge of water into the quiet rim of the pool beside the gravel bar.

His feet struck bottom. He took two stumbling steps toward shore, gasping from the cold and the shock. The pool was cutting a hard, chill line just at the V of his buckskin shirt.

The Sioux stepped to the edge of the gravel with his gun half raised. Bennington recognized it as an old English trade musket. The Sioux's round, hard eyes were both wide open as the rifle came against his shoulder. They did not change, but his lips went tight, and the start of that was the warning Bennington acted on.

He ducked deeply into the water. He could not hear. He had no way at all to judge the success of his timing, and so he had to come up almost instantly, either to meet the smash of the ball into his face, or to know that he had a little longer to live.

120

The warrior was just lowering the musket. A bloom of smoke was drifting away from the muzzle. Bennington brought his own rifle clear of the water. He allowed bare time for the water to run from the barrel before he pulled the trigger.

The hammer *snapped* and that was all.

He tried again. The second water-ruined cartridge was a brother to the first.

The Sioux, Hunkpapa he was, dark and happy now, tossed his rifle aside and put an arrow to his bow. He made a motion of drawing it. He grinned when he saw how Bennington tensed himself to duck. Underwater Bennington had shifted his rifle to his left hand. His knife was in his right.

He said: "Come out and fight me here." If he could get closer, he would throw the knife. He stepped ahead and felt the gravel bottom sloping sharply inshore. One more step and he would be floundering over his head.

The Hunkpapa answered with grim humor. "I am not a beaver, White Rain, who loves the Crows."

Bennington thought: *He knows who I am and he knows that I was camping with Stunned Elk's horse stealers.* Neither of the thoughts was helpful. The small party of raiding Crows with whom he had camped a few days while building the boat had thought him crazy. They had sat in the shade shaking their heads as he lashed the framework of the boat together.

Two days before it was finished they had gone down the Yellowstone on their ponies. Their opinion of Bennington must be right. No doubt they were alive and dry and healthy; he was up to his neck, fifteen feet out in the water, facing a war-smeared Sioux who didn't give a damn about counting coup on a live white man.

Bennington again invited the warrior to join him. It was only talk and they both knew it. The Hunkpapa's stone-solid eyes glinted as Bennington edged downstream and almost went under when he struck another sloped-off place. Bennington lurched as he regained his balance. He was trapped. The Sioux was well aware of it or Bennington would have been dead before this.

Strong and seething the river ran at Bennington's back. He could feel it holding his buckskins tightly against his body. He could twist sidewise and dive for the heavy current, let his rifle go, and try to swim out of arrow range. It was only a flashing thought; he was not that kind of swimmer. Before he was across the white water that had wrecked his boat, the Sioux would have him stuck up with arrows like one of the floating buffalo carcasses that Ree boys used for target practice on the Missouri.

Without raising his bow to full position, the warrior sliced an arrow close to Bennington. He grinned with broad humor as the white man ducked. It never paid to curse a mortal foe in combat. You taunted him, insulted him, but you did not curse him. Bennington could not help it; he was too scared. He cursed the Sioux in English.

He brought his knife up toward his chest. It would not be an easy throw because the water would impede his arm during the final quick jerk and cast.

"White Rain, who loves the Crows." The Sioux chugged another arrow close to Bennington, and then at once laid another shaft on the twisted string. The first two had been flint-headed. This third was a steel point, well serrated, faintly shining with bear fat.

The Indian had enough of sport. It never lasted too long with any of them. The arrow lay flat across the bow while the warrior told Bennington that he, a white man, had killed High Wound upstream. Now White Rain, who loves Crows, was going where all the soldiers had gone.

Bennington threw the knife. He made the cast half blinded by the explosion of water from the sudden surfacing of his arm. It might have been a good throw but the Sioux leaped aside with smooth, instinctive co-ordination of mind and coppery muscle.

He was done with humor now. He raised the bow and his lips began to tighten. Bennington saw the scars of the Sun Dance on his broad chest muscles as the bow ends bent back.

Bennington drove sidewise into the current. He went under and felt the sudden rip of the wild, cold power against him. He came up in spite of himself. He heard the rifle shot as the current shot him downstream. He tried to look back but the white waves slapped across his face, blinding him, strangling him when he gasped for air.

In spite of his efforts to dog-paddle across the current, the river dragged him with it. He shot another desperate look across his shoulder and this time, before the leaping water whacked the vision from his eyes, he saw a white man striding from the willows with a smoking rifle. The Sioux was down.

He heard another shot as he paddled high, like a swimming hog, splashing toward the tip of the gravel bar.

CHAPTER
TWO

Otis Dameyer made a fine figure of a man as he stood on the bank watching Bennington diving to recover his rifle. Dameyer was all the way from St. Louis on some kind of Army business that he had hinted at before he shut up, as if he did not trust Bennington.

Up from his third dive, Bennington rested, as well as a man could rest neck deep in water with the cold soaked all the way into his marrow bones. Dameyer looked like an officer, all right, Bennington judged.

He was big-framed and lean, with a cavalryman's flat-muscled legs. His eyes were a bold, staring blue. His hair was dark bronze. It appeared that he had trimmed lately with scissors the curling tightness of his short beard. He had a wide mouth with full lips, the kind that can go in an instant from ready humor to cruelty.

"You might have dropped it out in the current, Bennington," Dameyer said. "Try farther out."

He talked like an officer, too, Bennington thought. Nobody was going to recover a rifle out in that current, but it was not there; it must be closer inshore, somewhere in the deep pool just beyond the strip of high bottom.

Three dives later Bennington found it. He come up sputtering and cold-weary, and splashed toward shore. Dameyer was dragging the dead Sioux toward the water.

"Leave him there!" Bennington reached the shore and staggered up. The sun instantly made him feel ten degrees warmer.

"Why?" Dameyer asked.

"It won't hide anything to dump him in the river. The Hunkpapas will know we got him anyway." Give any dead Indian a right to be borne away and scaffolded by his friends. Pushing the water from his shaggy black hair, Bennington watched Dameyer's face and knew instinctively that the man would not understand.

"How do you know he's a Hunkpapa?"

That would be hard to explain to Dameyer, too, so Bennington said — "I know." — and let it go at that.

Bennington looked at the Sioux. That second shot had come from Dameyer's pistol, a wasted shot, and just now Dameyer wanted to throw the warrior into the river.

In the willows the big gray horse came forward to meet Bennington. The saddle was Sioux and so were the nose hitch and war rope. The brand on the hip was a big *US*. Bennington removed the saddle. Along the back and barrel of the horse the marks of a McClellan saddle were still worn into the hair. He raised the mount's hoofs one by one. They were still well shod.

"One of our horses, of course," Dameyer said. "I shouldn't be a bit surprised if they got him when they butchered the paymaster's guard a few weeks ago near Bismarck. You heard about that?"

"No." Bennington put the saddle back on the horse.

"How long have you been out?"

"Over a year."

"I see." Dameyer smiled. "Then you wouldn't hear much about Army news, of course."

"Not a word." A poor year, unless you figured experience worth something. Bennington had been close enough to the Pacific to trade for a pack of sea otter skins that would have put St. Louis buyers on edge. The Blackfeet had the furs now.

He led the horse from the willows. Out in the white water the rock was clean again. His rag of a boat had torn loose and floated away. Whoever had told him he was a boatman?

"Over a year, eh?" Dameyer said pleasantly. He lit a cigar. It was so out of place that Bennington stared at it resentfully. "You've really lost track of civilization."

"I'll catch up when I hit Fort Lincoln."

"Former Army man?"

"Yes."

"Confederate cavalry, no doubt?"

Bennington looked at the teeth of the gray. Six years old, he guessed. "So my accent still sticks a little, huh?"

"Quite a little. Louisiana or Mississippi?"

"I was a private in the Iron Brigade, the Second Wisconsin." The 1st Brigade of the 1st Division of the 1st Corps. Why was it every damned fool he met had to assume he had been in the Southern Army just because he was a Southerner?

127

"No offense, Bennington." Dameyer was persistent. "You still act cavalry to me. After the war?"

"I was in the Seventh, yes."

"Fine regiment." Dameyer was relishing his cigar. "They were camped on the Heart River when I came out. I stopped with them overnight. I knew Colonel Benteen during the war." He found another cigar and gave it to Bennington. It was not manners; it was more like a bribe.

After the weird Indian mixtures Bennington had been smoking, the cigar tasted good. The gray horse pleased him; it was transportation that would not go sidewise the instant he quit steering it.

"How did you like it?" Dameyer asked.

"Like what?"

"Service with the Seventh?"

How, indeed? Bennington had ridden since he was five. That part of it was fine, but that was very little of his service. Most of it was boredom, waiting, regulations that galled after the easy discipline and hard fighting unity of the Iron Brigade. For being drunk one night below New Fort Hays, Bennington had been put in the guardhouse pit, on orders of Colonel Custer.

Bennington remembered the pit, a hole in the ground, banked over with poles and dirt. He had spent five days there. That was part of service with the 7th Cavalry, too.

He answered Dameyer's question. "It was all right, if you like the cavalry."

"It so happens that I do." Dameyer studied Bennington from bold, blue eyes. "It's about mess time. Let's eat and talk something over."

★ ★ ★

Bennington was cleaning and drying his rifle when Dameyer brought two horses from the willows downstream. The way the pack horse was laden, it looked as if Dameyer intended to go all the way to the Columbia without shooting game. Twenty feet from the dead Sioux the two men cooked and ate.

"I'll stand obliged for some hardtack and bacon," Bennington said. "Enough to take me down to Lincoln on the gray."

"You're not taking the gray. It's government property. You're not going down to Fort Lincoln anyway, Bennington." Dameyer was rock-tough one instant, and the next moment he smiled as if apologizing for his harshness. "I think you'll change your mind when you hear what I have to say."

The Army never changed wherever you encountered it. Bennington watched Dameyer recover his cigar from a log where he had placed it while eating. The end was chewed into a long, twisted mess. Dameyer cut it off with a hunting knife and relit the stogie.

"There was about twenty-five thousand dollars in the payroll wagon old Sitting Bull got a few weeks ago. At least it was some of Bull's warriors, we're sure. They may have thrown the money away by now. Again, maybe not. My job is to find out and to recover any part of it that's left."

"Some job," Bennington said.

Dameyer watched him coldly. "The Army thinks it's worth a try. The Sioux have no use for money, probably don't know the meaning of it. They killed the

129

paymaster's guard and looted the wagon in hopes of finding arms, perhaps. At any rate, we know they carried off the money."

"Near Bismarck?"

Dameyer nodded. "It's scattered on the prairie from there to the head of the Missouri."

Bennington looked out at the river. He was anxious to be on his way.

"I'm ordered to go right to Sitting Bull himself to see what can be done," Dameyer said.

"That was an easy order for somebody to give. Do you know where he is?"

"We heard the White Rain Mountains," Dameyer said. "I'll be frank with you. I had an Army scout with me until I told him what the orders were. He turned around and rode back." There was shrewd opaqueness in the round blue eyes. "It wasn't all chance that brought me here in time to save your hide, Bennington. I've been watching you for two days."

It sounded like a lie to Bennington. "How so?"

"Two days ago I met the Sioux you were camped with when you were building your boat. Old Stunned Elk could talk a little English and I can work by hands fairly well. He told me you'd be coming down the Yellowstone any time, if you lived to make it." Dameyer smiled. "You barely did."

If you were any good, you did not keep reminding a man that you had saved his life. Possibly Dameyer did not know any better. He certainly was ignorant in other things, almost unbelievably so. Stunned Elk's bunch were Crows. Dameyer had called them Sioux.

The Army had chosen a green apple for an impossible task. Bennington looked Dameyer over carefully, as if he had not seen him right the first time. The man had a tough, sure cast to him, without doubt. That he had come this far alone proved that he was determined to carry out his orders, even if he did not know a Crow from a Sioux.

Army stubbornness was fine, but it also could get you killed in a hurry.

Bennington said: "Did you reload that rifle after you shot?"

Surprised at the sudden veering, Dameyer stared at Bennington, and then he colored slightly. "I didn't, for a fact." Then he defended himself. "I still had the Colt."

"Sure." Bennington picked up the war rope of the gray. "Sitting Bull may be in the White Rain Mountains, or on the Rosebud, or clear up on the Marias." He shook his head. "How about the hardtack and bacon, Lieutenant?" Dameyer was no lieutenant and Bennington was sure of it.

"Captain Dameyer," the man said gently, automatically. He watched Bennington's hand on the war rope.

He had not been a captain very long or he would not be so conscious of the rank, Bennington thought. Just how far was he going with that bluff about not letting Bennington have the gray?

"That's government property, mister. I'll need that horse." Dameyer did not reach toward his pistol. His voice did not rise. "The supplies I can spare you, but not the gray." He was cold-blooded and well poised; he was not bluffing.

131

Bennington could make a fight of it and take the horse. It would be a bad fight, too. He might have to hurt Dameyer. He kept looking at the officer and knew it would be worse than that; he would have to kill Dameyer to get the gray. After all, the man was going in and Bennington was going out. It did not make sense to fight a fellow white man, and an Army captain in the bargain, over a government horse.

Bennington thought it over. When he was sure that he was not backing down, he dropped the war rope.

Dameyer showed no expression of triumph. "You've been out a year. Why not another week or two?"

"It's a crazy job. You're wasting time, Dameyer."

"Couldn't you find Sitting Bull's Oglallas?"

Hunkpapas, damn it. "Sure, I could find Sitting Bull." Be taken to him, rather. You never *found* a particular Indian in this forbidding country.

"Well then?" Dameyer said.

It was all very simple to him. He was an Army officer acting on orders. Orders were all right when someone with sense gave them. Dameyer would go blundering on and get himself killed.

"I know you can do it," Dameyer said. "Stunned Elk told me that you were one of the best . . ."

"Yeah, sure, me and Charley Reynolds and Yellowstone Kelly. No thanks, Dameyer."

"That's odd. Lonesome Charley Reynolds was the scout who turned back on me."

"He was smart."

Dameyer shrugged. "Take the gray, Bennington. I'll get along." He walked over to his pack horse.

132

The order-dedicated, Indian-ignorant idiot was going through with it. Maybe he was a fool but you had to hand it to him for having guts and determination. And he had not tried to prod Bennington with any hints about being paid as a scout. Bennington looked at the captain's rifle leaning against a log, still unloaded. Wasn't that something? Yet, except for that rifle, Bennington would be lying dead somewhere along the gravel bar, with his legs in the water, with a round area gleaming on his skull.

CHAPTER
THREE

Dameyer was digging into his pack.

"Never mind," Bennington said. He got on the gray and started upriver. He had always been somewhat of a fool himself.

Captain Dameyer came along behind him without a word. Dameyer showed no triumph. He acted as if he had known from the first that Bennington would go along with him. With brass and confidence like that the man would be a brigadier before his hair was gray.

The Sioux that Bennington had pumped through the stomach was not dead. He lay where his companion had dragged him, and his horse, a mean-looking blue pony, was still close to him.

"Well, by Judas!" Dameyer said, when he saw the Sioux's eyelids flicker over the gray haze that was beginning to deaden the dark brown of his eyes. He drew his pistol.

"Put that away." Bennington got down and knelt beside the dying Sioux. The glazing eyes cleared for an instant as hatred swept the cloud away. "Sitting Bull. Where is he?" Bennington asked in Sioux.

The Indian's eyelids flickered. He got his hand on his knife and there was still a little strength in him as he struggled to keep Bennington from taking it out of his hand. When his wrist failed, the Sioux tried to bend his head down to bite Bennington's wrist.

"No use, Dameyer." Bennington stood up.

Dameyer still had his pistol in his hand. He shot the Indian in the chest and the warrior gave a small, conclusive jerk.

Bennington swung around angrily. "You're alone the next time you don't listen to me."

"He could have crawled away and got well. Look what happened when they shot Rain-In-The-Face and bayoneted him and left him for dead . . ."

"You'll listen to me from now on, or I'll take that pony and you can go it alone."

Dameyer began to reload his pistol. "You're the scout. I'll listen."

Bennington led the pony close to the Sioux. As a gesture of respect to the warrior he wished to kill it, but he did not like the idea of another unnecessary shot. He tied the pony to the willows. Other Sioux would be here before long; the land was swarming with them.

Until dusk Bennington set a fast pace. They were between the Rosebud and the mouth of the Big Horn River. Just before dark they crossed the Yellowstone, went over two long ranges of dry hills, and camped at Red Springs. Bennington was uneasy then. They had not seen an Indian all afternoon, or any fresh sign.

Dameyer wanted a fire. Bennington said no, and there was no fire. In the dark, making a long tour around the camp, he almost stepped on a rattlesnake that sent its dry, deadly warning as Bennington leaped sidewise in the deep grass. The incident shook him all out of proportion to its importance.

Dameyer was in his blankets when Bennington went back to camp. Dameyer was not worrying about anything. He yawned and said: "All quiet, huh?"

"Quiet enough for us to lose our horses. I'll stand the first four hours to midnight."

"Fair enough."

"Where did Lonesome Charley turn back?"

"About twenty miles out of Lincoln. Why?"

"Was he all right? He wasn't sick, was he?"

"No," Dameyer said. "He told me it was a fool's mission."

It was, too. "Who assigned him to you?"

"Colonel Custer, of course." Dameyer yawned again.

Charley Reynolds was not the kind to turn back for anything less than extraordinary reasons, but maybe he had thought Captain Dameyer was reason enough. No Army scout was forced to take idiotic orders like a soldier. Still, it worried Bennington.

It did not worry Dameyer at all. He went to sleep in five minutes, snoring like a fat hound. Bennington kept thumping him with the toe of his moccasin, making him turn over. Between going out to the horses and trotting back to keep Dameyer's snores from being heard by every restless Sioux in Montana Territory, Bennington spent a bad four hours.

He did not trust Dameyer after the first watch was over. For a while Bennington lay awake in his blankets. But Dameyer stayed alert. He went out to the horses. He moved around without too much noise. Bennington went to sleep. Four hours a night was about all either of them would get from now on.

At 4:00 in the morning Dameyer was ready to go on. Whatever else he lacked, he had toughness and an eagerness to do his job.

They quartered away from the rising sun, riding the long, rolling hills. It was a big and lonely land they crossed and it seemed to be uninhabited. Bennington had seen it that way at times, but he had never accepted a clump of trees, a thicket, the willows beside a stream, or any other cover at face value.

"Who said Sitting Bull was in the White Rains?"

"Scouts. Bloody Knife and some of the others Custer seems to trust so much."

It did not matter. The White Rains were as good a place as any to head for. They would find Sitting Bull when they ran into Sioux who were disposed to, or who could be persuaded to, take white men to him. Some of it depended on the fact not being known that the two of them had killed High Wound and the other Hunkpapa.

In the afternoon they were fifteen miles from the Yellowstone, going southwest toward Tullock Forks. Bennington held it unlikely that they would reach the Little Big Horn without running headlong into Sioux.

He kept wondering about the marks of wood cutting he had seen late yesterday afternoon. While they were still on the west bank of the river, he had looked across the swift water and had seen where trees had been chopped on the east bank, even cottonwoods that burned poorly in steamboat fire boxes. Dameyer had been ducking branches and hustling the pack horse along. Bennington doubted that he had observed the marks across the river.

"How long were you at Fort Lincoln?" Bennington asked.

"Several days."

"Did any steamers go up the Missouri?"

"I heard that the *Far West* left from Fort Buford sometime last month on Army business."

"To the Yellowstone?"

"Up the Yellowstone, they said."

The *Far West* was nearly 200 feet long. It could be handled on the Yellowstone, Bennington guessed, but it would be a mean and dangerous task. He asked: "Where was it headed?"

"I haven't the least idea," Dameyer said. "I'm only a dumb captain."

"What outfit?"

"The Sixth Engineers."

Engineers! Bennington said it under his breath like a curse. They could corduroy a road through a swamp or maybe get some sort of boat bridge across a river, but what did they know about Indians?

If Captain Dameyer observed Bennington's disgusted reaction, he gave no sign of it. Dameyer rode along in obvious enjoyment of the country, relaxed and easy, smoking a cigar. He acted as if the sight of 100 Indians rocketing down suddenly from the next bare ridge would not even give him a start.

I'll find out about that pose before this is over, Bennington thought.

He found out soon.

138

There were about twenty-five in the bunch. Dameyer and Bennington came upon them unexpectedly, if you could call a quarter of a mile a distance "coming upon". It was close enough. There were men, women, and children in the bunch. Immediately there was a furious stirring of movement.

The women and kids went at a run up a ridge. Bennington saw a child fall from a travois. An old squaw with her gray hair streaming dropped off a calico pony and scooped up the child, running with him.

Bennington saw a headdress blossom suddenly on one of the warriors milling between him and the fleeing squaws. Two of the bucks cut off at a high lope to gain the top of a knobby hill. The others seemed to be racing aimlessly, kicking dust in all directions.

It was a heap of activity for the size of the alarm — two white men sitting their horses quietly on a ridge. Bennington made the peace signal. He said: "Just sit, Dameyer. They're coming."

"Good!"

Bennington shot the captain a quick glance. The man was not scared. Maybe he didn't have sense enough to be scared. Bennington watched the signals of the two warriors who had gained the knobby hill to see what kind of support lay behind the white men. They sent the truth down to the others. The others let out long, quavering cries and came on in a rush.

"What kind of Sioux?" Dameyer asked. He might have been asking for information to put in a report, for all the emotion he showed.

"Don't know," Bennington answered. He swallowed slowly. He and Dameyer had excited the band far too much for normal circumstances. He saw the feathers in the tails of the ponies as the Indians came charging.

"Sit quiet," he said. "Don't get excited."

Dameyer's voice held an amused tone. "Take some of that medicine yourself, White Rain."

The Indians split their charge, winging out on both sides of the motionless white men. In the center, the chief with the headdress shouted — *"Hi-yi-yi!"* — in a drawn-out, trembling call that carried far across the hot, dry hills.

"Musical bugger," Dameyer said, and Bennington wished he would keep his mouth shut.

Bennington looked from side to side. The flankers were obeying; they were watching their chief. For the moment at least everything depended on the man with the headdress.

The chief slowed his pony from its flashing run. He shifted his rifle and raised his arm, and then he dropped down to a walk and came up the hill toward the white men.

They were Cheyennes, Bennington saw then. The chief was Blue Buffalo. Three years before Bennington had seen him in the camp of the Oglallas, with whom the Cheyennes were strong brothers. Bennington dropped his hand and made the signs, and said: "I am glad to see Blue Buffalo once more."

CHAPTER
FOUR

For just an instant his use of the chief's name raised little sparks of surprise in the Cheyenne's eyes. The warriors crowded in, dark with suspicion and hatred. Magnificent physical specimens, they were, the tallest and the most clean cut of all plains tribes.

One of them reached out to snatch Dameyer's rifle. Without moving the weapon, Dameyer shook his head, smiling. His eyes were like round rocks and there was no fear in him. The warrior wheeled his pony back. His companions laughed. The warrior raised a Springfield carbine.

Dameyer said harshly: "We have seen too much blood. Blue Buffalo says it."

The warrior lowered the carbine and rode to the outer edge of the group. Across the hills the squaws had stopped and were looking back, with the dust of their flight settling around them.

"We are in peace," Bennington said. "We would speak with Tatanka. We have heard he is in the White Rain Mountains."

Blue Buffalo was willing to parley, but he did not get down to go through the usual ceremonies. Urgency was in him. It might be, too, Bennington thought, that guilt was riding him. At least he was not at ease. His eyes moved with a sharp kind of worry as he followed Bennington's casual glances at certain equipment of the warriors — five or six Springfield carbines, shot boxes of Army issue, a sergeant's chevrons on a patch of torn blue cloth tied in the tail of one of the ponies.

"Tatanka is gone," the chief said.

"Where has he gone?"

Blue Buffalo pointed. "Down the Rosebud, beyond the Yellowstone. Far away."

Another warrior slammed his pony in close to Dameyer. He held a knife close to the captain's face. With that and the dark stare of glittering eyes he tried to strike terror into Dameyer.

Dameyer grinned pleasantly. "Put that away, bucko, or I'll drop your guts in your lap with it."

The warrior did not understand the words but he understood the fearlessness of the captain. Blue Buffalo grunted angrily and waved the buck aside. Blue Buffalo said to Bennington: "You are scouts for Man Without Hip?"

For General Terry. Bennington shook his head.

"For White Whiskers?"

General Gibbon. Bennington shook his head. "Alone we seek Tatanka to speak with him."

Once more Blue Buffalo pointed north and east toward the Rosebud. He started to turn away.

One of the Cheyennes said angrily, pointing at Bennington: "He rides the horse of Stab Bear!"

"Before that it was the horse of the Great White Father," Bennington said, "and now it is his again." He gave the Cheyenne a hard stare. It was a bad moment. There were no rules to judge Indian behavior. The Cheyennes could catch fire and rub him and Dameyer out in moments. Bennington slid his hand back and rested his thumb on the hammer of his rifle.

Blue Buffalo put his pony around again. Fury glittered in his look as he watched Bennington, and then the heat began to die. He became sullen, discouraged, almost afraid. He waved for his warriors to follow him.

They did not have to obey him. They put their savage hatred against Dameyer and Bennington. A small, quick move, a tiny crack of fear in the white men and the thing would have exploded. Lacking either, one of the warriors could have boiled over anyway.

Dameyer threw contempt like words from his odd blue eyes. Bennington sat quietly with his hand on the rifle, with his face grave and steady, with all his fear jammed down where it did not show.

"There has been too much blood," Blue Buffalo said.

The Cheyennes listened to their chief. As they rode, away, one of them smashed in close to the white men and lashed the pack horse so that it jumped and tried to break loose. The warrior who had turned back from grabbing Dameyer's rifle swerved his pony and struck the captain across the shoulder with a string of scalps.

Dameyer smiled faintly. "The next Sioux I shoot in the guts won't get a mercy shot."

It was not worth saying that the band was Cheyenne, not Sioux. For a man who knew little about Indians, Dameyer had stood up to their bullying tactics like a

143

veteran. Maybe it was not so important to know one tribe from another. Maybe the Army knew its business, after all, when it sent Dameyer.

But Bennington was not obliged to like him; a man without fear was inhuman.

"What did they say about Sitting Bull?" the captain asked.

"We're going the wrong way."

"Maybe they lied."

"Maybe they did." Bennington turned the gray and started across the hills toward the Rosebud.

Dameyer followed him. "They'd been in a scrap against our cavalry, did you notice?"

Bennington grunted. How could he have missed noticing? Three Springfield carbines, odds and ends of cavalry equipment, but there had not been an Army horse in the bunch. Blue Buffalo was headed toward one of the reservations. Before he reached there, the carbines and other Army gear would be well concealed.

Blue Buffalo had been ill at ease. There had been guilt in that repeated talk about too much blood already. Whatever kind of skirmish the Cheyennes had been in, they had won, or else they would have been in a much uglier mood.

"Did the Sioux burn that payroll wagon?" Bennington asked Dameyer suddenly.

"No. Why?"

"I'll bet they burned it. There went your money, Dameyer. We're risking our hair over nothing."

"They took the money, be sure of that. All we have to do is find out how much of it they hung onto."

Dameyer squinted at the distance ahead. "How far to the Yellowstone?"

"We ain't even to the Rosebud yet." For some reason, despite Dameyer's actually being a pleasant man, Bennington wanted to quarrel with him. He could not name the quality of character that irritated him. It wasn't entirely Dameyer's bold, almost insolent disregard of danger, or his flashes of arrogance, but they were part of it. It must be, Bennington decided, a deep coldness in Dameyer that was difficult to describe and not always readily apparent.

Bennington remembered something that had flashed in and out of his mind while they were waiting for the Cheyennes to come up. "Where'd you get my name . . . White Rain?" He used the Sioux words.

"From Stunned Elk's bunch."

"Tell me something about Stunned Elk's braids, Dameyer."

"One of them was turning gray. The other was still mostly black." Dameyer chuckled. "It gave him a lop-sided look."

That was Stunned Elk, sure enough, but the Crows had their own name for Bennington. Cha, Wolf Hair. "You didn't get my name from Stunned Elk, Dameyer."

Dameyer gave the impression of shrugging. "Where are we likely to run into Sioux again?"

"Anywhere," Bennington answered curtly. The Hunkpapa Dameyer had killed by the river had called Bennington by name, at least twice, but Dameyer was not supposed to understand Sioux.

Bennington tested that supposition. "You heard Stab Bear use my name, Dameyer."

"Stab Bear?"

"The Hunkpapa you killed."

"Stab Bear, White Rain." Dameyer chuckled. He found two cigars and tossed one across to Bennington. "Sure, I heard him. I understand enough Lakota to catch a few words now and then. It's like letting people think you're stone deaf. You hear a lot that you wouldn't catch otherwise."

"If you were that near, you sure shaved things close before you shot him."

"Didn't I?" Dameyer met Bennington's angry stare with good humor. "It was a funny sight, you'll have to allow. You up to your ears in the water, the Sioux slicing arrows at you . . . I got him in time. What more do you want?"

They struck the Rosebud the next morning. Bennington had gone up it in June the year before when the delicate odor of wild roses filled the whole valley. Now there was the biting smell of hot dust raised by the horses. Suddenly Bennington asked: "What month is this?"

"July." Dameyer calculated. "The Thirteenth. July Thirteen, Eighteen Seventy-Six." He smiled to himself.

Of Indian sign there was plenty. All along the way the grass had been grazed down by ponies. There were campsites where lodge poles still stood. The staked circles and the fire pits were weeks old, but the enormity of the campsites, strung for miles along the river, made Bennington uneasy.

146

Thousands of Sioux had ridden here this summer. The unshod hoofs of their ponies had pounded a trail hundreds of yards wide beside the stream. There were marks of shod horses, too, widely dispersed among the more blurry outlines of the plains ponies. Cavalry even under the most careless of lieutenants on scout did not spread out like that.

Bennington rode with a tingling down his spine. He was not positive about the picture he was reading here, but it seemed to have an ugly look. When they stopped to rest the horses at noon, he found an Army canteen under a bullberry bush.

"Some careless recruit will pay for that," Dameyer said.

"I'd say he already had."

As usual, Dameyer switched his position when there was no point in carrying on pretense. "The Indians have run off a batch of Army horses, for certain, wouldn't you say?"

Bennington looked out at the marks of plains cavalry that had passed in numbers greater than the strength of some corps he had seen during the war. He was tired of jostling words with Captain Dameyer of the 6th Engineers, who said the obvious or lied beyond comprehension.

They made twenty-five miles that day and were still about twenty-five miles from the Yellowstone when they camped.

Again Bennington took the first watch, sitting in a clump of bushes far enough from the Rosebud so that the sound of it neither lulled him nor dulled his ears.

Tonight Dameyer slept silently. Even the horses were unusually quiet.

It seemed to Bennington that the host that had passed up and down the valley was all around him now in the ghostly starlight, not threatening but riding by in endless strength, going to some appointed place.

The pale set stars and a sensing of time slipping through the barrier of midnight told Bennington when to rouse Dameyer, who came from his blankets instantly alert.

Dameyer pulled on his boots. The breech of his Springfield made light metallic sounds as he put in a fresh cartridge. Then for a moment he was stockstill. "It's strangely quiet, isn't it?" His voice was a murmur.

"The Indians are long gone from here." Bennington believed it, but still he felt the presence, the ownership, the flowing splendor, and the dark savageness of a people whose mark would be forever on the land.

"Tomorrow we'll find them," Dameyer said.

"We're weeks behind this migration." Suddenly Bennington had a hope and a wish that Captain Dameyer would give up when they reached the Yellowstone again.

"Weeks, then," Dameyer said. "We'll find them." He rose and made a tall, broad shape against the night. He walked confidently into the hushed darkness to take his post.

CHAPTER
FIVE

In the morning Dameyer was eager to move on. Bennington had never seen a man so anxious to find Sioux. Bennington himself had lived among them when circumstance forced him to do so, but he had never considered them blood bothers, or even been entirely at ease in their camps. Captain Dameyer was fairly busting to get right in the middle of the most bitter of all the Sioux, the bands from all the seven councils, the fiercely independent dissidents who would have no peace on white men's terms, who followed the harsh counsel of Tatanka, Sitting Bull.

All the way down the Rosebud, Bennington looked moodily at the fat U marks of steel-shod horses sprinkled among the tramplings of thousands of ponies. It was no small scout detail the Sioux had rubbed out to get those horses. Of course it was possible that each horse did not represent a dead cavalryman; the Indians might have stampeded the mounts of several companies engaged in a skirmish.

He asked: "Did soldiers go up the river from Buford with the *Far West*?"

"I think so," Dameyer said. "A few companies of cavalry pacing along on the bank, some of the Sixth Infantry on the boat itself. Why?"

It was always *why* with Captain Dameyer. Bennington did not answer. He kept searching out the marks of shod horses in the wide trail.

"That's not our business," Dameyer said. "Forget everything but the orders."

Now it was *our* business and *our* orders as Dameyer assumed that Bennington was solidly stuck with the detail. That was not the case at all; Dameyer just might lose a second scout when they came to the Yellowstone.

Out in the chopped swath where the Indians had ridden, Bennington stopped to look down on torn strips of faded blue cloth. Squaws had used them as diapers for their infants. The sun pressed hotly upon his back. The land was big and empty. Those pieces of cavalry blue, used like an insult, cast here in the dust, seemed to express the shocking hatred of the Sioux for white soldiers.

Dameyer said: "How far to the Yellowstone now?"

"We'll get there soon enough."

They came upon a dead horse, a cavalry mount with the McClellan still on it. Bennington got down and walked around it. The horse had been shot in the head at close range. He stepped close and lifted the canteen on the saddle. It was empty. The horse had bloated and popped and now the flesh was sagging away and the yellow teeth of the animal made a long snarl.

Dameyer gave it a glance and said: "Let's get on." A mile farther on he pointed to the left. "Let's cut across

150

to the islands. We can make an easier ford there, rather than following the Rosebud all the way down."

That was so but how did Dameyer know it? He had given the impression of being lost ever since Bennington met him. "The Sioux stayed with the Rosebud," Bennington said.

"Bully for them. Let's cut off toward the islands. We'll find the Sioux if we just keep riding in their general direction." Now he was the martinet condescending to explain his order.

He was right but Bennington still wanted to be stubborn. His dislike of the man had grown to where it overshadowed his puzzling about Dameyer's character.

"Is there any particular advantage in staying right in the middle of this Indian 'pike?" Dameyer asked.

Bennington led the way off to the west, toward the islands in the Yellowstone. They came to the river, and Bennington stopped to cool the horses before making the crossing. He said: "We've gone in a circle, almost. How'd you know these islands were here in the bend?"

Dameyer broke off a handful of willow tops and tried to rub the dust from his high Wellington boots. "Good Lord, man, I rode past the islands on the way to find you. Besides, I've got a map."

"I might let you depend on that map from here on."

Dameyer smiled. "Another boating expedition, eh?"

"No, I'll ride."

"Do so if you wish." Dameyer squinted across the river. "What's the best route for me to take after I cross?"

151

He could be bluffing but it did not seem so. With a singleness of purpose that was at once admirable and enraging, the captain was going on with his assignment. Money taken from a paymaster's wagon. Dust scattered on the wind.

Bennington felt like cursing but he knew he was going to stick. At the first, if he had known how much of a liar Dameyer was, he would not have gone with him. Clever liars were generally also clever cowards, but Dameyer was a combination that utterly stumped Bennington.

"We reach Sitting Bull, say. All you're obliged to do is get some report of what happened to the money, is that it?"

There was a hard challenge in Dameyer's stare. "Are you suggesting something else?"

"You don't expect to recover any of the money, do you?"

"I do, if they've got any of it. Every note goes back to the government. Were you hinting at something else?"

Bennington had not been hinting at anything else. He had been trying to estimate the length of their stay in Sitting Bull's camp, in case they ever got there. For his part he wished to visit the Sioux as briefly as possible. Dameyer had taken a different meaning from the question. Just how genuine was his outrage? Bennington said: "You'll see that I get paid as a scout?"

"I'll try. That's all I can promise."

No amount of money was worth the risk that lay ahead. If Dameyer had made at any time glib promises about Bennington's being rewarded for his services,

Bennington would have distrusted him, but now the officer's blunt honesty in the face of his own need of help settled Bennington's mind.

Sun glint from the water bounced in Dameyer's crisp bronze whiskers as he mounted. Bennington studied out the first island. It was covered with a dense growth of willows and the upstream end of it was strewn with débris from floods. Most of the heavy water was on the far side, for the stream between here and the island was shallow enough to show bottom.

The river was less than belly deep on the horse as Bennington approached the island. He was turning to see how Dameyer was coming with the pack horse when he saw a small movement in the willows.

There was one Sioux, crouched low. He rose as Bennington turned his rifle to bear on him. Then there were a dozen Indians who rose suddenly to full height from the willows. Bennington saw the rifles, the war arrows steady on the bows, the grim, dark faces.

Even devoid of paint they were the most murderous-looking band of Oglalla Bad Faces Bennington had ever encountered. Their coppery skins were gleaming wet from the swim to the island. The white men had stumbled into the trap with no resistance, so that for a moment the Sioux were at a loss. It would not last long, their lack of design.

Fear rocked up and down in Bennington, but his face was grave as he rested his rifle across his thighs and said: "We seek Tatanka Watanka." Most of the fierce dark eyes were on Dameyer. The Indians were hoping he would try to fight or run. Without turning Bennington said: "Don't try anything, Captain."

Dameyer's answer was as cool as the river. "I guess we found them, didn't we?" He came splashing on and several warriors waded out to meet him. They cut the tow rope of the pack horse. They punched at the pack, testing for loot, as they brought Dameyer ashore.

A brawny warrior grinned at Dameyer. He said — "Friend." — and reached his hand up, and like a fool the captain reached down to meet the gesture. The next instant the Sioux jerked him from the saddle. They pounded him brutally while they were taking his weapons. They kicked him to his feet at last and turned to Bennington, closing in around him.

"We are in peace. We are not scouts. We have come from the White Father to speak to Tatanka," Bennington said.

"Tatanka does not speak to mice," said one.

"Tatanka sets the hoofs of his pony on mice," said another.

"And on white man soldiers," said a third.

"Tatanka does not know the White Father," added a fourth.

"He will speak to us. The White Father has sent us. We are only two. We are here," Bennington said. That they were still alive was because it had pleased the Oglallas to let them walk straight into a trap. The Sioux were not given to making captives of grown white men. Bennington and Dameyer would die here or they would go to Sitting Bull's camp as visitors.

Still on his horse, Bennington knew that he held a small advantage. When they dragged him from it, the gates of savagery would swing wide open and he and Dameyer would die quite simply. He glanced down at Dameyer. The captain's face was bloody. The roughing up he had taken had roused a horrible temper in him, and now, with attention centered on Bennington, Dameyer was sizing up the chances more from the standpoint of anger in him than from logic.

"I will not argue with children," Bennington said. "We have come to see the Water Pourer, whose medicine is powerful. He has dreamed already of our coming. He will be displeased if his dream is violated by careless children."

One of the warriors growled: "Hear the big words of this white man, this mouse whose heart squeaked with terror when he saw us."

"Let the white scouts swim to the next island while we shoot our arrows at them," said another.

That suggestion fell sensibly among the Oglallas; there was little sport in clubbing to death two enemies who had offered no fight. Several warriors grunted approval of the idea.

"White Rain has said his words." Bennington gave the warriors a contemptuous look, and then he raised his eyes to look above their heads, as if they were miserable objects who did not concern him, but from the edge of his eye he watched Dameyer.

Dameyer was not as hurt as he had pretended. Dameyer was reaching under his shirt. The idiot had some kind of small handgun there. He was pulling it free when Bennington swung his rifle. The barrel cracked down on Dameyer's head and the captain buckled at the knees.

The sudden move startled the Sioux. The warriors close to Dameyer fell back. Bennington dropped from his horse quickly and took the wicked little handgun away from Dameyer. A big Oglalla stepped in to crush the captain's head with a war axe. Bennington shoved him back with an open hand.

"My friend is a child, too," he said. Bennington tossed the handgun down. "We have come to see Tatanka!" he shouted. "We have had enough of your foolish acts!" He glared around him savagely, letting anger hide his fear.

The Sioux went into council. Two of them had recognized the gray horse. They were in favor of killing the white men without further delay. Older warriors ruled against them. After all, White Rain had spoken of a dream. Tatanka had many dreams. Perhaps White Rain had spoken with a split tongue, but it was not safe to disregard dreams. Better to let Tatanka Watanka decide if the white men were liars.

Dameyer lurched to his feet. All the heat was out of him and the shrewd determination was in his face again. "I almost ruined it, didn't I? Are they taking us to old Bull?"

"We'll see." You could not figure out the captain. He was the strangest mixture of fire and ice Bennington had ever known. At least his head for once had been put to a good use.

The Bad Faces took the white men's weapons. Two of the younger warriors started to loot the pack and were stopped by Clouds Floating, a scarred Oglalla who seemed to have the most rank. It was he who told Bennington: "We go to Tatanka."

"What did he say about Sitting Bull?" Dameyer asked quickly.

"They're taking us to his camp."

"We did it!" Dameyer's confidence was back with a surge.

CHAPTER
SIX

Three warriors took the horses across swift water to the next island. Dameyer was a miserable swimmer, also. Bennington saw him plunge in without a trace of fear but a moment later the captain was in trouble. Two young Sioux rocking along in the current beside Dameyer laughed at his spluttering and his frantic efforts to stay afloat. They let him almost drown before they grabbed his hair and towed him ashore.

Dameyer choked and gasped, but when he was able, he looked at the two warriors and grinned.

In the cottonwoods on the west bank five young boys were watching the ponies. Angry because he had missed the fun, one of them jabbed Bennington in the rump with a knife choked down at the point between thumb and forefinger.

Bennington knocked him heels up in the air and turned away before the youth landed. The Oglallas laughed.

Dameyer said: "I see there *is* a proper time to lose one's temper, after all."

Bennington glanced at a bugle hanging on the saddle of a young Indian's pony. There were two blood bay horses in the bunch, shod horses with government brands.

"You know what, Bennington, I'm going to pay you directly one hundred dollars from the payroll money. That's a whole month's pay for a scout."

Bennington gave the captain a narrow, disliking look.

For three days they rode northward with the Sioux. They crossed the Missouri and continued on into country that Bennington did not know. When they crossed the trail of a Crow war party, five of the warriors and three of the young boys went after their ancient enemies.

Late on the fourth day Bennington saw the Sioux camp ahead. It was the largest he had ever seen. Clouds Floating let out a shout and went zigzagging ahead on his pony. The rest of the escort, stolid with their importance, took Bennington and Dameyer on at a steady pace, ignoring the shouted questions of young men watching the pony herd.

Bennington held to a solemn expression as he made a quick estimate of the number of big cavalry horses in the herd. There were at least 200. He gave Dameyer a bitter look, but the captain's eyes were on the camp.

The excitement Clouds Floating had raised by his approach, the signal that he had found white men, was dying away as the Sioux escort took Bennington and Dameyer past lodges of the Minneconjou, Brulé, and Sans Arc. On ahead, set apart from all the others, Bennington saw a yellow council tent.

A group of chiefs stopped the escort and asked questions. Bennington recognized Gall, in whose camp he had once spent a month. Black thoughts were setting behind Gall's face as he looked at Bennington, who gave the signs that he was glad to see the chief again.

Gall turned away. Behind him banks of stone-faced warriors stood silently, their faces bad. And it was that way as the escort took the white men on through the camp, a bad quietness and a hatred showing starkly in all the Sioux. The chiefs now walked ahead of the cavalcade and the crowd closed in behind.

They passed lodges of the Cheyennes. Bennington saw Little Chief, the tall, thin-lipped orator, who folded his arms and stood impassively, giving Bennington no recognition whatsoever. When they came to the Hunkpapa lodges, a squaw and an old gray-haired woman pushed forward. They put their hands on their mouths as they stared at the horse Bennington was riding, and then they both broke into a loud wailing, sawing the air with their arms and rocking their bodies forward.

The keening lament of the women of Stab Bear, dead beside the Yellowstone, broke with a rawing effect on Bennington's nerves.

Captain Dameyer swung his head from side to side and watched the camp with high contempt. It was the right thing to do, but he was not acting, and therein laid another dark bundle of worry for Bennington — the Sioux understood acting and could admire it, but a genuine contempt of them was a deadly mistake. There were 200 cavalry horses in their pony herd at this moment because someone had shown contempt of a great, free people.

They came to the red and black lodge of Sitting Bull. Tatanka stood before it with Rain-In-The-Face, whose eyes were glowing with cruel, sharp intelligence. Rain-In-The-Face was standing by aid of a stick crutch and Bennington saw the queer hanging of his foot, as if the toes only could touch the ground.

Bennington said: "The White Father has sent a soldier and White Rain to speak to Tatanka Watanka." He gave the marks of respect to Sitting Bull.

The down-drooping lips of the Sioux's greatest medicine man tightened. The deep lines running from the corners of his bold nose grew stronger. His cloudy eyes looked at the white men as if they were pieces of spoiled meat. Sitting Bull had grown gray listening to the broken words of white men.

He turned his back and went into his lodge. Hobbling on his crutch, Rain-In-The-Face followed him. A feral rumbling came from the Sioux.

"That was the old boy himself!" Dameyer said excitedly. "Tell him to come back out here. Tell him . . ."

"Shut up," Bennington growled. He watched Gall and Bad Hip and Little Wound go into an impromptu conference. Clouds Floating stood aside, glowering angrily, as if he had been reprimanded for bringing the white men into camp. Sitting Bull had turned his back upon them, and now their position was worse than precarious.

Dameyer did not observe this at all; he started to complain again about Sitting Bull. He stopped when warriors grabbed the bridles of the horses and led them away. Bennington took a deep breath. Gall had saved their hides, Pizi, the irreconcilable, the white man hater, the true, hard man of the Sioux.

Inside a lodge guarded by the *akecita*, the Indian police, Bennington stood between the door flap and the fire pit and fought down a desire to kill Dameyer with his bare hands. From what he had learned from Clouds Floating, from what he had seen in the camp, the cavalry horses, the great number of wounded Sioux, Bennington had pieced together a grim and ugly picture.

Dameyer sat down on a pile of buffalo robes. He started to pull off his boots. "Give me a hand here, will you?" When Bennington did not move, Dameyer lay back on the robes and sighed with utter relaxation. "You wouldn't believe it, but I'm a little tired. When will we have the council with old Bull?"

"We never will," Bennington said. His voice was calm. "You start telling the truth or I'm going to kill you."

Dameyer started to smile, and then gave proper assessment to what he had heard, and his face grew sober. "I think you've guessed the truth, Bennington. You came along of your own free will, so don't act like a Puritan now."

"You'd better talk, Dameyer."

162

The captain bunched a robe under his head to gain more comfort. "The cavalry had a couple of scraps with the Sioux. Crook got his nose bloodied. Custer lost half his command, about three hundred men, over the Little Big Horn. He got killed himself, by the way."

"I said I wanted the truth!"

"You're getting it. You damned fool, do you think any man is immortal? Custer lost five companies of the Seventh, right down to the last man. Reno and Benteen took a bad mauling but the infantry came up the river in time to save them."

The casualness of Dameyer's words made Bennington say: "You're no officer. You never were."

"That's right," Dameyer said agreeably. "I'm a man looking out for himself, the same as you. There was no paymaster's wagon robbed near Bismarck. You guessed that before we started to cross the Yellowstone the second time."

I didn't, Bennington thought.

"But don't fret yourself," Dameyer went on, "there's money here for us. All we have to do is talk Sitting Bull out of it, and that can be done."

"What money?"

"The Seventh was paid about a month before the fight. They never had a chance to spend a cent. Most of that money is right here in this camp, Bennington. Figure the privates at thirteen dollars, about three hundred of them, average the officers' pay at . . ."

Bennington turned away with a sickness in him. He stumbled to the door of the lodge and looked out directly at a Fox warrior standing guard twenty feet

163

away. Beyond the Sioux a group of curious children were watching the tent. One of them had a rag on a willow stick. It was the lower bar of a swallow-tailed pennant, a blue bar with the handles of crossed sabers standing against it in white. Bennington had seen it many times, George Custer's personal pennant . . .

Dameyer was still talking and his words drained Bennington's strength like a knife plunged into his back. "Even if half of it was thrown away or lost, we still can figure on several thousand dollars. It's nobody's money, Bennington. The Indians have no use for it. I've got an idea of what to tell them about it, but you'll have to make the spiel of course."

The warrior waved the children away. They trotted off, shouting, and the blue bar waved and flapped on the stick.

Bennington grasped the sides of the opening, gathering the hide in a grip that made his knuckles stand white. He looked over his shoulder at Dameyer. "You filthy, miserable bastard."

Dameyer began to search under his shirt. "Right at the start I saw that you were soft inside, Bennington."

Bennington walked as far as the fire pit before the sounds of the village around him brought him control.

CHAPTER
SEVEN

"That's right," Dameyer said. He relaxed again and his fingers began to tug at the thing he'd been probing for under his shirt. "We're stuck. We've got to work together. What we think of each other has nothing to do with the problem." His smile was engaging. From under his shirt he pulled two cigars wrapped in oiled silk.

"These are the last, Bennington." Dameyer tossed one across the lodge. It struck Bennington's shirt and fell into the fire pit.

"Here's what you tell them, Bennington. Those green pieces of paper they took have the names and identification of the soldiers they killed. They chopped the dead to pieces . . . you know how Sioux perform. Tell old Bull that the White Father" — Dameyer's mouth curled with dry amusement — "has to know who his dead soldiers are, so that he can do them honor. The only way he can tell is to have the pieces of green paper." Dameyer lit his cigar. He lay back on the robes again with his hands behind his head. "It ought to work, don't you think? The Sioux honor their dead enemies, and we're not asking for anything that's useful to them."

With all his anger drained away and only a sense of helpless wonder left, Bennington stared down at Dameyer. *Who spawned such men? What kind of blankness was inside them?* "It might work," Bennington said tonelessly.

"Good! Then we're agreed. A third of the money goes to you. That beats a hundred dollars, doesn't it?"

"Yes, it does." Bennington walked over to the door flap again.

"When do you suppose they'll have a council? Tonight?"

"Likely." No matter what kind of slime had been forced on him, Bennington wanted to stay alive. He would use his wits and lie with a grave expression, assuming that the Sioux chiefs granted him the right to speak before them.

He looked through the doorway, past the *akecita* guards, on to the free hills beyond the stream where the camp was set. On the Little Big Horn — Custer wiped out? It was not possible. There had been fighting, yes, and the cavalry had been hurt, but . . .

A tall Cheyenne came by with a hunting party that was blood-smeared. The Cheyenne stopped to ask one of the guards what was going on. Bennington kept staring at the horse the tall Cut Arm rode, and, when the hunting party went on, Bennington stepped out to follow the horse with his eyes. A Fox warrior forced him back inside with a lance.

Bennington had seen enough. The sorrel was one of Custer's favorite horses, white-stockinged all the way around, a blazed forehead. Its name was Vic.

166

Bennington looked at Dameyer. With the cigar gone dead in his teeth, Dameyer was sleeping peacefully. Snoring.

Somewhere in the valley of the Greasy Grass near the bright blue loops of the river, was it? Bennington knew the country well. He and Dameyer had been almost there when they turned back to the Rosebud after meeting the Cheyennes.

In the evening an old squaw whose hands were mutilated from mourning her dead brought food to the lodge and went away without ever looking directly into the eyes of the white men.

Dameyer roused, refreshed and confident. He retrieved the cigar that had fallen from his mouth while he slept. He picked the other cigar from the fire pit and put it inside his shirt. "Well, they're not trying to starve us, eh, Bennington?" He ate with his fingers and sucked the juices from them afterward and once more asked when the council would be.

Darkness came and there was a council. Bennington heard the crier going about the camp, an old man with a deep voice. "Two white soldiers who fought against us on the Greasy Grass have come into the camp to speak to Tatanka, who will not hear their words. The chiefs will council. High Wound and Stab Bear, of the great Hunkpapas, have been killed by these two white men."

The crier went away. A silence came upon the camp. Bennington heard but faintly the distant counseling of the chiefs. Quite likely Sitting Bull was not with them, or else he listened in silence, for he was no longer a warrior. His power came from dreams, from the slyness of a great intelligence, but in the end life or death for Bennington and Dameyer would be largely Sitting Bull's decision.

After two hours the council ended. No one came for the white men. Dameyer said angrily: "Tell these guards we want to talk to Sitting Bull."

"You tell them." Bennington pulled off his moccasins and went to bed.

He had never slept completely relaxed in an Indian camp. He knew when the guard changed, and later he was aware of the man who came toward the lodge and held a low-voiced conversation with the *akecita*. The flap scraped back and the man came into the darkness of the lodge. He spoke Bennington's Sioux name.

"I hear." Bennington threw off the robes.

"Why are you here?" the man asked.

The darkness gave gravity to the lie Bennington told about the payroll of dead soldiers on the Greasy Grass. At first it was all a lie, and then it became mixed with truths that fell simply from Bennington's lips. He told the visitor that the quarrel of the White Father with the Sioux was one thing, and that the honoring of dead on both sides was another thing.

"The White Father did not send us to say that there will be no more fighting, or ask the Sioux not to fight again. We are not chiefs. We are only men. With the pieces of paper we will know the dead. We will honor them. This is all we ask of the Sioux, who honor their warriors who die bravely."

There was a long silence from the man who stood before Bennington. Meager starlight came through the

168

smoke hole of the lodge but it was not enough to reveal more than the gloomy outlines of the Sioux. Doubt rode the Indian's silence.

"These pieces of paper are traded among white men as ponies are traded among my people," the visitor said.

The man was making sure that Bennington did not mistake him for a simpleton.

"It is so," Bennington said. "The pieces of green paper are used among white men to buy what they wish from each other, but if the paper is returned to us, it will be used only to honor the soldiers who were killed."

Again the long silence ran before the dark figure spoke. "Five suns ago a dream was told in this camp. In the dream four white men were seen riding to the camp. They came to say that the White Father wishes peace, that the soldiers even now hunting for the Sioux will be sent away. You have not said this. You are only two. Where are the other two?"

This time it was Bennington who was long silent, with his mind racing over the implications of the statement and the questions. When the visitor first spoke, he had been reasonably sure of his identity, and now he was certain. Bennington asked a bargaining question of his own. "Will White Rain be heard by council?"

The visitor grunted in the affirmative.

Bennington took his time. His next words would trap him hopelessly if he had guessed wrong, or they would save both him and Dameyer. He said: "The dream was good. There were four white men sent. One turned back from fear. The other grew so sick with boils upon his back that he could not ride. Two are here. The others were chiefs and the White Father had told them to speak to the Sioux, to say that the soldiers would be sent away, to say that peace would be. I am not a chief and my friend is not a chief. We were to ask only for the pieces of paper to honor our dead, but I know what the others were to say and so I will say it to the council. The dream was good."

After a moment Sitting Bull turned swiftly and ducked through the lodge opening and was gone.

"What was that about?" Dameyer asked quickly.

A bargain? Yes, surely it must be a bargain. Tatanka was no chief. He was not even a warrior. There were Sioux who said he had no heart for fighting. It was known that he never went into battle. And yet he was the strong man of the Sioux and ruled a large number of them through a mixture of intelligence and medicine.

Dameyer said: "Who was that? What did he say?"

"I thought you understood some Sioux."

"Not the way you two grunted it. Who was it? Did you ask him about the money?"

"It was Pte. He said he would see about the money."

"Pte?" Dameyer asked. "Sitting Bull is the man we want."

"Pte is sacred to the Sioux." Buffalo were not only sacred but very useful to the Sioux. Bennington got back into his blankets. It was not luck that he had struck upon an Indian dream as an argument when

Clouds Floating and his bunch had taken him and Bennington. Indians lived by visions.

Sitting Bull was full of dreams based on logic, or one might say that where the dream ended and logic began, a fine line lay almost indiscernible. After the great victory of the Sioux over the 7th, was it not natural that white men would come to the Indians to talk? Sitting Bull had seen that this would be so, and, if he had presented it as a result of a vision, rather than the work of a shrewd mind, that was his business. Let him stand secure as a man of true visions. After all, he had missed but slightly the number of emissaries presumably sent by the White Father. Bennington was willing, even quite anxious to establish the lie that Tatanka had not missed the number at all. In fact, Bennington's life depended on it.

"Did this Pte say we would get the money?" Dameyer asked.

"He said the council would hear us."

CHAPTER
EIGHT

They were taken in mid-morning to the meeting of chiefs outside the yellow lodge. The Sioux war leaders had already passed through their ceremonies. No pipe was offered the white men, no gestures of respect. They came as beggars to be heard.

Bennington had a long bad moment when he looked at the hostile faces, Rain-In-The-Face, Kicking Bear, Pizi, the great, straight man of the Sioux, Crazy Horse, Bear Rib, Bad Hip, Little Chief of the Cheyennes, and many others.

Sitting Bull was there, dressed in a black and white calico shirt, his strong legs wrapped in leggings of black cloth, his cloudy eyes showing nothing, his gray hair running down to frame his broad face into narrowness.

The Sioux gave Little Chief the honor of speaking all the wrongs long held against the white man by the Sioux and Cheyennes. The list was long, his voice was good, and, when he made a killing point, the ranks of Sioux standing in hard quietness behind the council growled their approval like a chant. After a long time Little Chief wanted to know why two white men had come here.

In the strong daylight with the unwavering eyes of a fierce people upon him, Bennington found the lie hard to tell, but he told it with all the power and imagery he could muster.

The council listened. They were not impressed by the White Father's need of small scraps of green paper to tell the names of his dead soldiers on the Greasy Grass.

Bennington knew that he had to do much better. He spoke of the dream. "When we left the fort on the river, we said among ourselves that our coming was known. Tatanka Watanka sees that which others do not see, and so we were sure that he would know of our coming. There were four of us. One grew sick and fear overcame the other. Two of us are here. The other two were to speak of peace. I do not know everything they were to say and so I will not make up words, but I do know that they were to speak to Tatanka and the chiefs about peace."

Bennington saw belief come to the faces of the Sioux. It was simple for them to believe what they had heard already from Sitting Bull. Behind the chiefs the listening warriors shifted their eyes to the medicine man, paying respect.

Sitting Bull showed nothing. His eyes were drawn down tightly. His thin upper lip jutted slightly over the lower. He sat with his arms crossed and he gave the impression that he had heard nothing.

There was no more for Bennington to say. He looked above the Sioux, beyond the pony herd, out to the tawny hills. He was sweating. He waited.

Kicking Bear said: "We will consider the words of the white man." He looked to Sitting Bull, who held his withdrawn pose, not hearing.

Pizi motioned to the picked warriors of the *akecita*.

They escorted Bennington and Dameyer back to the lodge.

Dameyer was in a raging worry. "Sitting Bull never opened his mouth! What happened? Do we get the money?"

Bennington sat down on his robes. "We'll see."

"You're cool enough about it. Did you purposely foul up everything? I wish to hell I'd brought somebody I could trust!"

"What really happened to Charley Reynolds, Dameyer?"

"He was killed on the Little Big Horn. You didn't swallow *all* the lies I told you, did you?"

"I'm afraid so." Bennington rose and strode to the lodge door. Once more he found himself gripping the teepee hides so hard that his wrists and forearms began to ache.

The guards went away before noon.

A short time later the procession started. No warrior or even a toothless old man joined in it. Squaws and children walked past the lodge, throwing money through the doorway. There were handfuls of notes crumpled like the sprouting leaves of rhubarb. Some of the money had been smeared with filth. An ancient squaw with a face like a frost-wrinkled apple stopped in the opening, spat upon a bill, and let it flutter to the dust.

The fire of a wolf pup burned in the eyes of a young boy who swung back his arm and hurled a piece of colored cloth wrapped around a rock. It struck against the back wall of the lodge, a cavalry guidon, crumpled and dirty. Bennington picked it up, looking at the bloodstains on the circle of gilt stars.

A Cheyenne girl who could have been no more than three threw down a toy pony made of buckskin with a $10 bill tied on it as a saddle blanket.

Dameyer's eyes were alive and darting as the money began to litter the lodge floor. He snatched up a wallet with worn gold initials on it and a ragged bullet hole through it. There was money inside, a thick sheaf of notes stuck together with dried blood. Dameyer took the notes and dropped the wallet into the fire pit.

A hag with live coals for eyes thrust her withered face inside and started to hurl a scalp with a $5 bill tied in the hair. Dameyer snatched it from her hands before she had a chance to throw it.

The long line ended. Indian boys brought the white men's horses before the lodge, with all their possessions on them. Dameyer was on his hands and knees scrabbling around the lodge. "Gather it up! Let's count it."

The amount was a little more than $2,000. Dameyer cursed. "They held out on us, that's what they did! Go tell Sitting Bull we won't leave until . . ."

"We're leaving," Bennington said quietly, "while we have the chance. They haven't got any more money. They told me they threw most of it away right at the battlefield."

"Over three weeks ago!" Dameyer said savagely. "We'll go there just the same."

"Sure."

Dameyer was stuffing the money into the big pocket inside his shirt. A map and an Army tinder kit took up too much room. He threw them into the fire pit. "I'll give you your share when you get me back to one of the forts, Bennington."

It was another week before they found the battlefield. Between tufts of reddish-brown grass the soil was white and ashy on the hills above the blue loops of the Little Big Horn. The wolves and birds had been here, and the wind and rain, so that the fluffy earth heaped in haste upon the bodies of the dead was mostly gone now.

Bennington got down and led his horse through the litter of rotting equipment scattered widely on the hills. Here and there were small heaps of McClellans and rifles with broken stocks, all partially burned; the bottoms of cavalry boots with the tops cut off, already starting to curl in the sun; horses sinking into the earth; empty cartridge shells spilled in the grass.

He did not count but he knew that he had seen almost 100 bodies that had been covered with sagebrush only as a burial gesture. There were soldiers here that he had known, but there was no way of knowing them now.

Higher up the hill Dameyer was searching furiously for money. Bennington went up to him and on beyond him to where the basket from a travois was staked down over a grave, the only real grave that Bennington had seen. This would be the burial place of Custer, the Yellow Hair.

"Keep looking, don't stand around!" Dameyer shouted. He plunged away toward a pair of pants hanging on a bush.

Across the basket of the travois Bennington looked down at the Sioux campsite on the other side of the river. It ran for miles. Someone had burned the lodge poles. Grass was already rising in the charred marks. "There were too many of us," Clouds Floating had said.

Bennington led his horse down the hill to Dameyer.

"The Sioux lied," Dameyer said. He was hot and sweating. "I haven't seen a single bill. You can't tell me that the other soldiers picked them all up. They weren't here long enough even to bury their dead. I tell you the Sioux lied, and you . . ."

Dameyer was looking into the muzzle of Bennington's pistol. With his free hand Bennington was pulling the cavalry guidon from under his shirt.

"What's the idea?" Dameyer asked.

"I've been wanting to kill you for a long time."

"You fool! I'll give you your third of the money."

What made a man like Dameyer? What was left out of his insides, or so badly twisted that he was incomplete? Musing, staring, with the pistol in his hand, Bennington shook his head.

"Half the money then!" Dameyer shouted.

With a slow motion Bennington tossed the guidon to Dameyer. "Pile it on that." He watched the notes

177

tumbling from inside Dameyer's shirt. He watched the man counting. "Put it *all* down there."

Dameyer was like a cornered wolf, but he saw the curious listlessness in Bennington's eyes. He obeyed.

The money lay on the stained guidon and on the ashy soil around it. Bennington tossed down his tinder kit.

"You're crazy!" Dameyer shouted. "No, I won't!"

"Burn it."

"You're crazy!"

"Burn it."

"That's senseless, Bennington!" Dameyer flung his arm in a wide gesture. "It won't help them. It won't help anybody." Crouched on his knees, he stared up at Bennington. "You've gone Indian. You're starting to believe that story you told the Sioux about honoring . . ."

Bennington cocked the pistol.

Death was all around Dameyer and death was looking at him. His hands trembled as he ignited the tinder. The guidon turned brown, then black. A small, red-edged hole appeared in it. The hole spread but there was no flame until the money caught fire. It burned with an orange flame, with little smoke, charring away slowly.

Dameyer stared down in anguish. His heart was truly on the ground, where the wisps of smoke were dying away. "Why did you do that, Bennington?"

With the pistol Bennington motioned for Dameyer to walk away from him. The man started. He swung around and cried: "To think that I saved your life!"

"I just saved yours. Get out of my sight, Dameyer."

Bennington rode away from the mutilation and horror. From a hill above the high bluffs on the river he looked back and saw Dameyer going toward the Indian campsite. He would look there for money. He would look forever for money.

When Dameyer was completely out of sight, Bennington began to feel free and clean once more. He turned the tired gray horse toward the Rosebud.

The Big Trouble

CHAPTER
ONE

He Cries saw his first white men at the end of the summer of many rains. Big Elk, his father, had taken his family far from the main camp of the Uncompahgre Utes for the fall hunting, and now the lodge was set in the aspens at the head of a big park with never summer mountains hard against the night sky.

Ai, it was good to sit by the fire and think of the buffalo he would kill tomorrow. He Cries fondled his juniper bow and the straight arrows of currant wood in their bear-hide quiver that his uncle, Jingling Thunder, had made for him that summer after the big fight with Arapahoes at Red Mountain. He Cries had never killed a buffalo, but here by the fire with his stomach full of antelope meat and with a warm drowsy feeling coming out of the night to him, He Cries was killing many buffalo.

He had seen the scattered herds that afternoon when he stole after his father, who had gone to hunt. But something had changed Big Elk's mind. Watching from a hill, He Cries had seen his father suddenly veer away from stalking a small herd of cows and ride straight toward the mountains. So He Cries followed to see

183

what game tracks had taken Big Elk away from the buffalo.

It was tracks of men, five of them. They did not wear moccasins, which seemed very strange to He Cries. They wore something else that crushed the grass and left sharp edges in soft ground. He Cries followed, fascinated, until Big Elk reached from the ambush of a spruce thicket and grabbed him by the breechclout.

He Cries was not caught entirely unaware, for he had seen where Big Elk leaped aside from the trail, and so the son had time to set an arrow and half draw his bow. That was fairly good; otherwise, Big Elk would have ignored his son for several days as punishment for carelessness. Big Elk asked, looking at the trail: "How many?"

"Five. They wear strange moccasins."

"They do," Big Elk said. "Go back to the lodge." His face was dark, so that He Cries was sure it was time to go.

Now Big Elk sat by the fire silently, with the darkness behind his eyes, such as the times after coming from councils where he had shaken his head at Arrow, subchief of the Uncompahgre Utes, who was no friend of Big Elk or his brother Jingling Thunder. He Cries's mother and her mother were singing the night song of the leaves, not loud, for that would not have been well, with Big Elk looking so darkly at the fire. He Cries moved a little closer to his grandmother. Old Running Woman, captured as a child from the Cheyennes long ago, was not like other old women who let their buckskin skirts grow black with blood and grease, who said only sharp words to those who married their daughters, and who were forever complaining that the hunting had been better long ago.

Running Woman's buckskins were clean and white, like those of He Cries's mother. She raised her voice when there were things to say, and she said them without fear, so that even Big Elk listened.

And now she ceased her singing and said across the fire: "What is it, my son?"

Big Elk looked at her half angrily. He did not like it when she read his mind and asked questions before he chose to speak. Her daughter was getting the habit, too, Big Elk often complained. There would be no peace in a man's lodge when he was old. He scowled at both women, and then looked at the fire again.

But Running Woman was old, and her face had been painted black many times for sons and nephews who came back dead across their ponies. She was old and had seen many things, and so a scowl did not bother her.

"Did you see the marks today of those with tattoos on the breast?" she asked.

Big Elk answered because he knew he would have to answer sooner or later. "The Arapahoes are gathered now in camps for hunting on the plains. They will not be in the mountains." He glanced at He Cries. "No, old woman, I did not see the marks of the Arapahoes."

He Cries felt his mother's hand touch him, then push against him gently. It was time for him to go into the lodge. The others would talk then about what Big Elk had seen this day. He Cries did not care. He was too sleepy. Tonight in his dreams he had many buffalo to kill, and tomorrow . . . perhaps . . .

His mother's hand ran down his back, patted him on the thigh as he moved away. Both she and Running Woman watched him go, but when he glanced back from the lodge flap, yawning, the three at the fire were staring at each other solemnly.

They had cloudy thoughts, He Cries thought. They did not seem to know that dark things that sometimes troubled the mind at night all passed away before the morning sun stood bright on the forests and the mountains.

Terrible thunder jarred He Cries from his robes. He sat up, frightened. There was no whispering rain against the hides of the lodge, and the flaps were not tied. It could not be raining.

From outside he heard Big Elk grunt deeply in his chest. The thunder came again, so loud, so close that He Cries clapped his hands to his ears. And then he heard strange voices running rapidly in an unknown tongue. His mother cried out fiercely. Running Woman began to sing. The grunts and blows of a sharp, brief struggle came to He Cries.

He crept to the lodge flaps and looked out. Big Elk was lying on his face by the fire, and the fire showed the bright streams running from two holes in his back. A man all covered with clothes was looking down at Big Elk, in his hands a long brown club that smoked. The smell of the brown club had drifted clear to the lodge, filling He Cries's nostrils with a bitter smell.

★   ★   ★

There were five of the men whose bodies were covered. Their faces were hairy, and by that He Cries knew they were what the old ones called white men. Three of them had the big sticks that smoked. Two were holding He Cries's mother on the ground.

Antelope meat was scattered on a buffalo robe near broken cooking vessels. They had eaten, these strangers with hairy faces, and then they had killed Big Elk. He Cries was filled with terror, but he half rose, ready to leap from the lodge and then he heard what Running Woman was singing.

Run, He Cries, run away.
Big Elk is dead.
Run quick, run far, He Cries.
Run to Jingling Thunder.

He Cries's mother began to struggle again, twisting against the hands that held her. She spat into one of the hairy faces. The man struck her as one kills a rabbit with his hand, and she lay still.

"Run quick, run far . . . ," the old woman chanted.

One of the men turned toward the lodge, speaking sharply in the strange tongue. The hair upon his face was as red as mountains that had just hidden the sun, and it seemed to He Cries that his eyes were red also when they saw the figure crouched at the flaps. The man raised the brown club, grinning, with firelight strong on big white teeth.

From under the wide fold of her skirt Running Woman snatched the juniper bow that He Cries had left beside her. She strung an arrow swiftly. The bow made a little *thump* and the man with sunset in the hair of his face shouted. He dropped his brown club and grabbed his arm, tearing at the arrow.

Running Woman started to set another little arrow. "Run, He Cries!" she said.

The awful thunder came once again before Running Woman could draw the small bow. Her head went low upon her chest and red blossomed on the white of her beaded dress.

He Cries ran with a sob in his chest. He wormed under the hide wall away from the fire and darted into the aspens. Two of the hairy faces came after him, crashing hard with their strange moccasins. In terror He Cries ran, forgetting everything Big Elk had taught him.

The white men sent their thunder after him. It reached out and knocked He Cries into a bush, filling his head with a great brilliance. But that was what saved him. He lay still then, holding one hand against his head where only part of an ear remained. The white men *crashed* close to him, shouting to each other, but he lay still, crouched like a snowshoe rabbit. After a while they went back to the lodge.

Just once as he was slipping away, quietly now, he heard his mother cry out. The last he heard was the loud laughter of the hairy faces.

He was naked in the cold night with the never summer mountains black around him. His head was still ringing from the thunder sticks, and the injured side was hurting. He whimpered a little.

It was at least one sun to where he had last seen Jingling Thunder's lodge, two suns to the main camp. He Cries swam a big beaver pond. He tore his legs on roots when he scrambled out on the far bank, and then he trotted through the tall grass, never doubting that he was going in the right direction.

He would remember till the day of the big sunset this night when he had seen his first white men.

He Cries was then five summers old.

His name was White Bear, after the great hunch-shouldered grizzly, the summer Arrow's people camped on the slopes below the Mountain of the Snow Woman. The boy who had been He Cries was gone, vanished with the little whimpers he had made thirteen summers before when he ran through the night from miners who had killed his family.

The wedge of dark brown hair that ran into a braid on the right side of his head did not hide his mangled ear. There were other scars on him now, for he had taken six scalps from the Tattooed Breasts. The blood of the tall Cheyennes had carried strongly down to him from Running Woman. He was lighter than the other Utes and taller by two hand spans than the average.

Today he was going to raise his voice in council.

Jingling Thunder came from his lodge, followed by his sons, Red Cow and Soldier. Strong of frame, almost black-skinned, Jingling Thunder had the same quick-fixing gaze that was all White Bear could now remember of his father. The years had not hardened Jingling Thunder's joints or put a film on his eyes. He could still ride hard and see a flick of movement miles ahead, just as long ago when he had ridden in one day from the headwaters of the Arkansas to the big white man's town upon the plains, trailing five hairy faces who had taken Big Elk's ponies.

White Bear's mother had been dead when Jingling Thunder reached the lodge at Bayou Salade. They were all dead, but White Bear's mother had not died a good death, and that had left a terrible bitterness against all white men in her son. The bitterness was shared by Jingling Thunder, who had missed catching up with the five by no more than the flight of two long arrows.

Jingling Thunder sent a wicked look toward the huge lodge of Arrow. There were two white men in there now, messengers from their big chief. The sides were not rolled up to catch the cool air, which was the case too often when white men came to talk to Arrow.

"They say one thing to Arrow. In council he says another thing to us." Red Cow spat. He sent an angling look through the piñons to where Shavano, war chief of the tribe, sat before his lodge with a sullen fierceness on his face.

"The white men promise things to Arrow, but they are not the promises we hear from him." Soldier spat and looked at White Bear.

"Silence," Jingling Thunder said. "Your voices are like the piñon birds." His face said that they spoke truth.

Red Cow and Soldier were warriors. They had ridden many times beside White Bear against the Arapahoes and the Striped Arrow people. They had been far south and brought back ponies and scalps from the Navajos. But their father's words kept them silent for a little while.

Then Red Cow spoke again. "The white men who wash the river sands and dig holes in the rocks are slipping back across the mountains every day."

"The last big party that Arrow took to the pass went only a short distance after he pointed eastward and said . . . 'Go.' Now they are traveling toward the San Juans once more." Soldier grunted. "That is the white man's way of keeping his promise."

"I know these things. Be silent," Jingling Thunder said. He looked at White Bear, who had not said anything. He did not have to, for long ago he had counseled for killing every white man who broke the word of their big chief that no more miners would cross the mountains.

White Bear had never changed his mind, but so far he had obeyed Arrow.

Shavano heaved up from his bone backrest and came to the group. He was as tall as White Bear, a wide man, with the hard, fierce freedom of the mountains stamped on him. On the war chief's broad face White Bear read all the things that he himself believed. Shavano was a fighter. His courage was like a rock. He knew that the coming of the white miners was like water creeping through the grass, just a sparkle of it showing here and there, until all at once the eye realized that all the land was flooded.

Shavano was no coward. He hated white men. But Shavano did not know what to do. True, he had counseled war, but every time Arrow said not war, but talk.

"The council will begin soon," the war chief said.

Jingling Thunder grunted gloomily.

"Old men talk," Red Cow said. "They talk and more white men cross the mountains. That is council."

Soldier spat. "The war trail is the answer to all talk."

Shavano's eyes flared dangerously. "When did Shavano turn from the war trail? When did Shavano show fear?"

"Never," White Bear said quietly. He looked at Red Cow and Soldier, shaking his head. He felt as they did, but this was not a thing to be helped by fighting among themselves.

Shavano stalked toward Arrow's lodge. Little children scrambled from his path. The women were silent as he passed.

CHAPTER
TWO

White Bear sat far back at the council before Arrow's lodge. As a subchief of the Uncompahgres, he was entitled to a forward position, but he did not care to be any closer to the two white men than necessary. One of them was a soldier, tall and brown as a plains Indian. Menzies was his name. He had ridden into the camp without fear. There was no hair on his face.

The second was a big man who had got from his saddle stiffly, with the water and color of the sun on his face. He had thick hair down the sides of his face and hair upon his upper lip. Although he wore no clothes to mark him as a soldier, it was said that he was a chief above Menzies. He was called Shallow.

White Bear sat straight, with the sun heavy on his back. There would be much talk, like wind in the aspen leaves, before anything was said. He watched Arrow.

Like White Bear, Arrow was not all Ute. His mother had been an Apache, and Arrow had spent many years in the south among the Spanish whites, so that he knew their language, as well as some talk of the whites who came from the grassy plains. Wide as a rock, hard as a thick piñon tree, Arrow sat with his sharp eyes watching everyone.

The soldier, Menzies, was speaking formal words of greeting to the council, talking slowly, stopping to think at times, but he knew the words. When he sat down, he spoke in his own language to Shallow, telling what he had said. Shallow smiled a little, and then he rose to speak.

White Bear did not like his voice from the first, although he did not understand the words. Shallow was not giving counsel; he was making threats. He punched with his fingers. They were fat and white. His voice was too sharp and loud. It reminded White Bear too much of other white men's voices on a night long ago.

Greasy Grass translated. He was half Sioux, half white, and had trapped many years in the mountains among the Utes.

"Kill no more white faces," Greasy Grass said. "Follow Arrow's way. Point them from the country and let them go in peace. The white chief promises that soon no more will cross the mountains." The interpreter swept his hand toward the Continental Divide.

"Soon!" Shavano grunted like a bear.

There had been one promise that the white men would stop crossing the first range of mountains. They had not stopped, and now they were crossing the second range to the sacred hunting grounds of the Utes.

"Arrow will be chief of all the Utes . . ."

There were startled grunts from many. Arrow was a subchief only because the Utes willed it. Who was saying he would be chief of all?

194

"Only with Arrow will the white chief make his treaties. Soon Arrow will go with his subchiefs to put his name on the talking leaves that will tell what part of the mountains belongs to the Utes and what part to the white chief."

White Bear was stunned. Since the first sun all the mountains had belonged to his people. In astonishment he looked at Arrow, who was undisturbed. Shavano's face was like a black rock. Jingling Thunder, old warrior that he was, had put one hand over his mouth in surprise.

"There will be meat and presents for the Utes," Greasy Grass went on. "For all the land they once owned there will be payment made every year. It will be done with Arrow."

Arrow sat. He said nothing. He did not seem displeased. He had known of this talk in his lodge before the council, White Bear thought. He had agreed to it, and he was only a subchief. No man among the Utes had the right to give away their land.

"But first," Greasy Grass went on, "those who killed the three white men on the Crooked River two moons ago must come forward. They must be punished."

"By the whites?" Shavano asked.

The interpreter looked at Shallow and spoke. Shallow nodded. He said many words.

Greasy Grass said only: "Yes, by the white men."

White Bear knew who had killed the three miners on Crooked River. Red Cow and Soldier and some other young men. It had been a fair fight. The white men had guns, and the Utes bows and arrows, and so Red Cow and the others had crept in at dawn and killed the white men before they could use their guns. Yes, it had been a fair fight. Soldier and another Ute had been wounded by the white men's knives before the fight was over. The Utes had not gone into the camp as friends, eaten the white men's food, and then killed them.

When no one spoke or moved, the one called Shallow rose with anger on his face. He started speaking again in his sharp, threatening voice, pointing with his finger.

It was too much. White Bear rose. The speaker stopped, his finger in mid-air.

"The messenger from the white chief says the Utes who killed three white men must be punished." There was mighty anger in White Bear, but he spoke carefully. "Thirteen summers ago white men killed my family. They also must be punished."

An angry storm came onto Arrow's face.

Shallow turned to Greasy Grass, who translated White Bear's words. Shallow shook his head, and, when his words came from the mouth of Greasy Grass, they said: "That was a very long time ago."

"Two moons, thirteen summers. Time does not matter. The white men must also be punished."

There were many grunts of approval, the young men making most of the noise.

Arrow rose, his face like thunder. "The white brothers come in peace," he said, looking at White Bear. "There must be peace."

Arrow was not afraid, White Bear knew. Like Shavano, Arrow did not want peace because he feared war. But Arrow must know that the mouths of white men ran on and on, while their hands reached for knives. That he must know, but the white man had spoken of making him chief of all the Utes, and perhaps that had caused his eyes to go blind. Perhaps Arrow had been blind for a long time, ever since he talked to white men alone in his lodge with the sides rolled down to earth when the sun was hot.

"Let the white men give to us for punishment those who killed my family," White Bear said. "Then we can give to him those who killed the men on Crooked River."

Menzies smiled just slightly as he looked at Shallow, who let his words run hard and quickly.

"That cannot be done," the interpreter said.

White Bear grunted scornfully. It was as he had thought. He pointed. "Let all white men stay beyond the mountains."

"My brother is angry," Arrow said. "White Bear thinks of long ago when bad men came into the country of the Utes and harmed his family. Now the white chief has promised . . ."

"Let his promises be done, not made by marks on the talking leaves. I have had enough of talking leaves that no one but the white chief understands."

Arrow's anger rose murderously. He had killed when anger was upon him like that, and now he would have fought with White Bear, but they were too far apart.

"I am the chief!" Arrow said.

"*Ai!*" White Bear smiled. "The white man's chief, not mine."

Arrow sprang forward, drawing his knife as he came. The council was in an uproar instantly. Shavano and Querno grabbed Arrow, and some of the other subchiefs helped. Jingling Thunder pushed White Bear back, scowling fiercely.

"The council is no place for fighting," he said.

"Talk. White man's talk." White Bear turned and walked away. From the hill where they had been watching, Soldier, Red Cow, and some of the younger men came down to follow White Bear toward his lodge. Menzies and Shallow marked well their going.

Arrow was still talking in council when White Bear and his party rode away. They took with them no more than they needed for the war trail.

"Where?" Red Cow asked.

"We will find the white men who slipped back across the mountains," White Bear said.

Soldier grunted happily. He felt the buckskin bag that held his war paint.

Munro Swallow, special representative of the Commissioner of Indian Affairs, and Captain David Menzies rode from the camp with Greasy Grass the next morning.

"It didn't take too well," Menzies said.

"It will. Arrow has to see that it does. He's bought."

Menzies squinted at the rocky pass ahead. "I wouldn't say that exactly."

"Call it anything you want. We set him up as chief of all the Utes. The government deals only through him. He gets an annuity. Ten thousand a year would be cheap just to have someone in authority with whom we can raise hell when it's necessary to our policy." Shallow laughed. "He'll be lucky if he gets a thousand a year."

"What is the policy?"

"Simple. We've known ever since Baker came out of the San Juans that the country is lousy with gold and silver. There'll be a treaty that says everything the other side of the Continental Divide is Ute land, inviolate." Shallow shook his head. "It won't stick, Menzies. It didn't in the Black Hills, and it won't here, and, when it starts to slip, we'll have Arrow under our thumb. In a way, it's better than fighting, which is about all those black brutes seem cut out for."

"You think one man can control all the scattered bands of Utes? Arrow's only a subchief anyway."

"We'll build him up as the chief. There'll be trouble, yes, but we picked the right man. He thinks well of himself." Shallow looked sidewise at the captain. "How would you like being a major general, Captain?"

"All right."

"Of course, but maybe not as well as Arrow will enjoy being the big boss of the Utes."

Captain Menzies kept one eye on Greasy Grass and the other on the country ahead. The half-breed was a first class scout, but Menzies liked to use his own eyes and judgment. And he had not forgotten the young Utes who had walked away from the council with White Bear.

Shallow rode heavily. The country meant nothing to him other than land to cross. He said: "In time we may even convince Arrow that he's a great, smart chief who foresaw the futility of fighting the white man. Once he has that idea, once he's taken our gifts, he'll have to go right down the line with us."

"Who's *us* . . . the Department of Indian . . . ?"

"It's a little more personal than that, Captain. I also represent a group interested in the development of mining in the San Juans."

"You'll help make a treaty that you know our side will break?"

"It's inevitable, Menzies. How many men would you need to keep prospectors out of these mountains?"

Menzies twisted in his McClellan to look at the long caravan of gray-topped peaks running from the Mountain of the Snow Woman. His eyes rested briefly and coldly on Shallow. "Not men, Shallow . . . corps."

"Exactly. One day the Utes will have to go. In the meantime, it would be expensive to fight them, and it would be impossible to keep prospectors and miners from crossing to where they know gold lies."

"Expensive to whom . . . the mining interests you mentioned?"

Shallow nodded, his face hardening. "And to the government, too."

"Which worries you most, Shallow?"

The red-faced man spoke quietly. "How old are you, Captain?"

"Thirty-eight."

"Brevet?"

Menzies nodded curtly.

"I can understand. I was a brigadier at your age."

"A lot of politicians were, fighting the Mexicans from desks in Washington."

Shallow's color deepened. "No need for us to get personal," he said. "No need at all."

They followed Greasy Grass into the first turning of red, sun-scorched rocks that marked the pass.

"What would you do with the Utes, Menzies . . . let them hunt and fish and camp for the next hundred years on some of the greatest mineral deposits in the world?"

"I don't know, but whatever I did, it wouldn't be with my mind on one thing and my tongue on another. That White Bear hit it when he said promises should be done, not marked on paper."

"White Bear and those other young whelps who walked out on the meeting are setting themselves against big trouble. I spoke to Arrow privately about them."

"I know," Menzies said. "And Arrow spoke privately to me about the last party Red Youman took into the San Juans. The Utes chased them out, but Arrow knows the party started back three days ago." Menzies watched Shallow carefully. "Where do you suppose White Bear and those other fire-eaters were going?"

Shallow stopped his horse. "My God! If they get Red . . ." He urged his horse forward again. "We've got to get word to the colonel!"

"Indian country over there, Shallow. Theirs by solemn treaty. Enter at your own risk, and the cavalry won't help you. Youman knows that. You knew it, too . . . when you sent him to map out mining claims that your outfit intends to snatch fast when the Utes have been chased and butchered."

Shallow was not surprised. "How'd you know I sent Youman?"

"Both I and the colonel have suspected it for sometime . . . your plan, I mean. You never heard of Youman yesterday when I mentioned his name. Today you call him Red and nearly fall off your horse when it dawns on you that he might be gobbled up by Utes. I hope to hell they get him."

"That's fine talk for a white man, an Army officer."

"Those with him . . . well, that's too bad, but they knew their risks. Red Youman deserves any Ute arrow that catches him. From what I've put together, I think it was he who wiped out White Bear's family a good many years back."

Shallow was not impressed. He was not even listening. "It will be serious if they get Youman," he said, half to himself.

Captain Menzies went on ahead to ride beside Greasy Grass. The interpreter had never been known to wash. One eye drooped evilly from an old knife cut that ran from his forehead to his chin. Sometimes he rode all day with no more talking than an occasional grunt.

Menzies preferred him to Munro Shallow.

CHAPTER
THREE

Twelve warriors rode away with White Bear. When they all knew where they were going, two of them who were nephews of Arrow stopped the group for council. White Bear was sick of council but he listened.

Sick Wolf, one of the nephews, said it was not good to fight the white man. "Let us war, instead, upon the Arapahoes," he said. "There is always one or two lodges not far from the Waters of the Great Spirit."

Soldier grunted and made the sign of cowardice. From the time of the first mountain the Utes and their plains enemies forgot all thoughts of fighting when they went to drink the waters of Manitou.

"The lodges of these Tattooed Breasts are not at the healing waters," Sick Wolf argued. "Only close by."

"You have been too long listening to your uncle, Arrow," White Bear said. "Go fight the old sick men of the Arapahoes. We ride against the white men."

Red Cow laughed fully in Sick Wolf's face and made the sign of cowardice.

Sick Wolf and his brother put their hands upon their knives, but they were afraid of Jingling Thunder's sons, so they only held their hands upon their knives and swore their hatred with their eyes.

"Go back," White Bear said. "Perhaps Arrow can get his white brothers to help you fight the sick ones at Manitou."

Arrow's nephews rode away, and with them went another whose heart was not strong.

White Bear was silent a long time as he led the war party up the pass that would take them to the Crooked River. He had made bitter enemies this day, both in council at the camp and just now. Making enemies among one's own people was not good; it held the cloudy thought of what would happen if Arrow's friendship for white men caused little divisions among all the mountain Indians, so that they could not stand together when they finally learned they all must fight or lose everything to the water already creeping through the grass.

They stopped on top of the pass and put on the green and red stripes of their war paint.

There were fifteen mounted white men in the party, with five animals that wore the iron moccasins. It made White Bear's heart sick to see how well they knew the country of the Crooked River, going the easy way, avoiding the bogs and little blind cañons where even Utes who did not know the country well sometimes had trouble.

Straight down the Crooked River they had gone, then turned at the right place in the sage, so that they would miss the big tumbling cañon where no pony could cross. They were going straight and fast for the snowy Spanish Mountains where others before them had washed the yellow stones from the rivers and dug the little holes among the rocks.

Scouting the old camps carefully, White Bear and Soldier saw with what keenness the sites had been chosen, where there was natural protection for the horses, yet two or three ways to escape, and still good cover to fight behind if the attacking force was large. They saw, too, where the guards had been posted, not drowsing by a big fire, but in the rocks and trees on four sides of the camps.

"He who leads these white men is not here the first time," Soldier said. He glanced at his horn bow. "They will all have guns."

There was not a gun in White Bear's party.

"*Ai*. And they are fifteen and we are ten," White Bear said carelessly. "When their camp is made, they are strong. When they are traveling, their scouts will be like eagles. But when they are making their camp, their minds will be on food and rest and other things."

Soldier nodded. "I am with you, brother."

"They will camp this night at the bright lake of the black rocks. We will be there first. From what we have seen, they will send their scouts ahead, then all around the place of camping while their fires are being made."

"You are wise like the coyote and the spider."

"Jorno and Saguache move like smoke against the clouds. Their arrows find the big rabbit of the plains in mid-leap. They will wait for the scouts."

"We will fight the rest from the trees and rocks around their camping place?" Soldier asked.

"We will rush on foot into their camp."

Soldier looked thoughtful, but after some time he said: "I am with you, brother."

It was as White Bear had said. The white men prepared to make camp that evening among black rocks in a little open space beside the lake. White Bear and seven young men were watching from the dark spruce trees. They could not spare a man to tend the ponies that had been left behind them in the trees.

Red Cow's black eyes glittered as he crouched with his bow before him, watching the big horses that carried the packs. It would be fun to kill the white men, but riding into camp with two of those large horses behind him would be better.

Soldier watched all movements of the white men. Three of them went to the lake to water the riding ponies, and they did not take their guns. A huge man with sunset in his hairy face sat on a rock and directed the others. He kept his gun across his knees. He would be a bad one, Soldier thought, one they must kill very soon.

Soldier glanced at White Bear, whose face was set like a stone

in winter. Until now, Soldier thought, he had not known how much White Bear hated white men.

Two scouts had gone ahead. Jorno and Saguache were waiting somewhere up the lake. There would be no signal when their work was done. They were to come back quickly then and help the others.

The three at the lake were almost ready to come back. Two of the pack horses were unburdened now, and a man sent them toward water with slaps upon their rumps. But he did not go with them, and the three at the lake would return soon and be near their guns. Did not White Bear see that? Soldier wondered.

White Bear had seen. But his mind was reaching far back to the days of He Cries, when he had crouched at a lodge flap watching a hairy face whose eyes looked red down the barrel of a rifle. Out there on the rock with the rifle across his knees was the same man. White Bear looked at the rest. He could not tell about them. It had been long ago, and only one of the five who had killed his family had become fixed in his mind. The red one must be killed very soon in the fighting.

At the lake the three horse handlers started their ponies toward the camp.

"No war cries at first," White Bear said, and sprang from cover.

It was a queer thing, like a dream, White Bear thought, because for several long racing leaps the white men did not see the dark bodies charging at them. Then one of the men at the lake saw. He yelled.

All the white men, busy in the camp, looked toward him and cost themselves another three long leaps toward death, but the big one on the rock did not look at the man who yelled. He looked instinctively toward the trees. He fired the first shot without rising, and off to the left White Bear, from the corner of his eye, saw someone strike the ground.

Then the Utes were on the camp. Three white men were down in the first hard-driving whisking of arrows.

Two of the three at the lake leaped on ponies and rode away. The third ran hard toward camp, drawing a long knife as he came. Red Cow killed him with his second arrow.

Straight for the red one White Bear sprang. The man was like a weasel in his quickness. He put a rock between himself and White Bear. His rifle made a sharp *clattering* noise. Then it threw its thunder again, so close to White Bear that its hot breath burned between his arm and breast.

White Bear struck with his knife, reaching hard, but the red one was out of the way once more. The knife swept down and broke upon the rock. White Bear heard the rifle *clatter*. It would speak again. He leaped over the rock and caught the warm, round barrel with both hands.

He was strong, with the shoulders and tallness of his Cheyenne heritage, but he could not take the gun from the red one. They were close to each other for a moment, their muscles rigid. White Bear saw the same big white teeth and the same reddish lights in the eyes of the man who would have killed him years before.

White Bear tried to twist the rifle down. It went down a little. Then he reversed his power and tried to whirl it from the red one's hands. But the man was wise, and his arms were like the butts of dried lodge poles. He was too strong.

Suddenly he let White Bear have the rifle, shoving it at him and letting it go, so that the Ute sprawled clear over the rock and fell upon his back. The red one snatched a short gun from his belt and raised it, and the white wings of death made their beating sounds in White Bear's ears.

The hatchet came from somewhere behind White Bear. It rang upon the short gun in the red one's hand. It knocked it from his grasp. The hatchet struck so hard against the man's breast that he should have fallen. But he only let out a great bite of air, then turned and ran like an elk.

"I am with you, brother. Are you hurt?" It was Soldier reaching down to help White Bear.

The air was gone from White Bear. There was blood upon his chest and a gray burn under his arm, but he was not hurt. He got up quickly, in time to see the red one leap upon one of the big horses and gallop down the lakeshore.

Saguache and Jorno came sweeping by on their ponies. They yelled that they had killed the scouts with two arrows, and then they rode fast down the lake after the white men who had got away.

There were five of them, counting the red one. Two of them still had rifles. One of them killed Jorno's pony with one shot, so Saguache turned and went back to him, and the two of them came back to the scene of the fight.

Red Cow was dead. He had fought well, the others said, but before the fight was over he had run to catch one of the big horses, and a white man had shot him in the head. Running Wolf was badly wounded. It was he who had fallen at the red one's first shot. No one else was hurt badly. They had come upon the camp so quickly, not shouting war cries, that they had caught the white men by surprise.

It was a great victory. But Red Cow was dead, so it was not a great victory after all, White Bear thought. And the red one had escaped.

Jorno and Saguache were gathering up the white men's ponies. Scattered on the ground and among the packs were many things, among them guns and the sound-making dirt that was used to make the guns speak thunder. Soldier brought the red one's gun to White Bear, and with it small shiny things with soft stone in the ends. Soldier had seen such guns far south among the Spanish whites, and said he knew how to make them speak.

But he would not try tonight. His heart was heavy because of Red Cow. He went around the darkening water, and they saw him climbing upward in the rocks to make his medicine to the spirits of the sky and of the earth. He would tell them of his brother.

They camped at the upper end of the lake. Long after the moon was gone White Bear sat alone by the fire. Soldier came then, bringing a small deer he had killed with an arrow in the moonlight at the edge of the lake. They roasted meat on sticks, not speaking. Saguache, whose stomach was always empty, was wakened by the smell and joined them.

"It was a great victory," he said.

Soldier said: "When the sun comes, I take Red Cow to the summer camp. It will not be good when Jingling thunder knows."

"Bad," White Bear agreed.

A voice came ghostly from the night, so that Saguache dropped his meat into the ashes and stood up trembling.

"Jingling Thunder knows," the voice said.

Little drops of winter touched White Bear's back muscles even after he knew it was his uncle who had spoken. Then Jingling Thunder came from the dark into the firelight as silently as the bird that has no nest.

After a while White Bear gathered his wits enough to offer his uncle meat. Jingling Thunder squatted by the fire, eating rapidly. When that was done, he wiped his hands in his hair and said: "Querno comes with twenty warriors to bring the young men back to camp. Arrow is angry. His nephews spoke of this with a forked tongue. Shavano would not lead the party Arrow sent."

White Bear said with heavy heart: "Now it is no longer talk. Arrow fights on the white man's side."

Jingling Thunder looked old and tired for a moment. "Rouse the young men. Let them eat and go farther toward the sunset place. I will stay here with the wounded one and Red Cow."

White Bear called the others from sleep. They began to roast meat, blinking at Jingling Thunder.

"After you left the council, it was said by the white man with hair upon his face that it is their chief's order that the sunset side of the mountains belong to the Utes. The other side is theirs." There was bitterness of Jingling Thunder's face.

Soldier said angrily: "We did not agree! All the Utes must agree!"

"They will agree through Arrow," Jingling Thunder said. He stared at the fire, and added: "Perhaps in time Arrow will see what we see now." His words were without strength, White Bear knew, because his uncle did not believe them himself.

"Do not kill white men who will go from our land," Jingling Thunder said. "Warn them first. Kill them only if they do not heed the warning."

"They are like Arapahoes," White Bear said. "They need no warning when they come into the mountains!"

"The white chief does not care if we kill the Tattooed Breasts," Jingling Thunder said, "or if they kill us." He rose to his full height, and looked sternly at White Bear. "Warn the white men first."

He was wise. He was not afraid. White Bear loved him, and so White Bear said: "We will warn them."

"Go now," Jingling Thunder said. "Ride far."

The young men were ready to leave as soon as they were on their feet. Some were still chewing meat. Others thrust parts of the deer into their breechclouts.

Jingling Thunder's last words made them look away from each other for shame. "In camp, even after victory, there must always be sleepless ones to see that no one walks to the fire without being seen or heard."

Jingling Thunder did not look at them again, or watch them go.

CHAPTER
FOUR

That summer White Bear's band kept the Spanish Mountains clean of white men. They ranged from the edge of the desert where the rivers became sand to the red waters of the Colorow. They were hard and lean. They moved by night as well as day. In a land of much meat they often did not stop for their bellies when on the trail of white men. Querno could not catch them.

Always, as White Bear had promised, they gave one warning. If their words were heeded and the white faces started back across the mountains, the band trailed them to see if they were honest. Sometimes the white faces lied and tried to steal back to where they had been digging, after they made a pretense of leaving. All but one of these last left their bones among the rocks or in the dark gloom of the forests. He who escaped was a big man with no hair on his face. He was like the white bear of the rocks in his fighting, using his arms like clubs after his gun was broken. At last he ran into the rocks where ponies could not follow, going so fast that Jorno, who was lean and like the smoke in lightness of his running, could not catch him.

"Perhaps it was well," Jorno said, after he returned winded.

High up in the rocks the white man paused to laugh and shout back insults in Ute. *Ai*, he was a brave man, and in a way he reminded White Bear of the soldier called Menzies.

When those who dug the holes and played in the sands of the streams did not take the warning, they died. White Bear taught his band to attack in the night, creeping in close and using only knives. They wiped out several camps that way, and some they cleaned out by killing the white men one by one when they grew too excited over their digging and wandered away from each other in the daytime.

None of the band, not even Soldier, cared much for the night fighting, although White Bear said many times that none of them had been wounded that way, while several of them had been hurt in day attacks.

They did not use their guns until late in the summer. They were afraid, because the first time Saguache tried to shoot his rifle, it knocked him over and made a terrible sound. Saguache ran in a circle for a while, holding his hands over his head. The barrel of the rifle had a split in it, like a drum skin that had been stretched too tight when wet.

Soldier, who was wise about guns, said the white men had put a curse on them, but that it would pass before the leaves fell. It was better not to use the guns until he was sure the evil spirit was gone from them.

The evil spirit left not very long afterward when they met a Spanish trader on the Piedra. Soldier made much talk with him about the guns, and had the trader examine all the rifles. Afterward, Soldier said the curse was gone, that they must not let dirt or mud get in the barrels of the guns, and that they must be kept clean by means of the cloth and iron stick he had stolen from the trader.

"I think you should have ben a medicine man," White Bear told his friend.

They used to guns on one party of stubborn white men not far from the dusty cliff ruins of the Old Ones. There were four white men. The band killed them all while they were running toward their camp. White Bear thought he killed two of them, because his rifle was a many-shooting one. He shot several times more than anyone else, but he counted coup on only one white man.

White Bear had eight scalps that summer.

Ai, the band kept the Spanish Mountains clear of the diggers. White Bear thought they had done well, especially since they had to hide from Querno's warriors who had come to take them back to camp, as well as search out white men.

Sick Wolf and Little Buffalo, Arrow's nephews, were with Querno and they worked harder than any to find the band. And one day Little Buffalo did.

He called to them one evening when they were camped without fire on the Animas. He was on the other bank of the river, out of sight in tall grass.

"It is Little Buffalo!" he said. "I have looked for you."

White Bear's band was moving away, spreading out in the gloom. They knew where to meet later.

"I am alone." Little Buffalo said. "I want to speak to White Bear."

It might be a trap. White Bear made the night bird signals for his band to keep on going. He stayed where he was.

"Come!" he called to Little Buffalo.

Soon Arrow's nephew came dripping from the river. White Bear let him wait in the darkness until he was sure no others were swimming behind him, and then he spoke softly, and Little Buffalo walked to him.

"You have done well this summer."

White Bear was silent.

"Running Wolf's wound grows well. He is almost strong again."

White Bear said nothing.

"The council was with Jingling Thunder. Arrow was afraid to try to punish him for warning White Bear's warriors."

That was glad news, but white Bear was silent.

"Arrow has gone with many subchiefs to the far lodge of the great white soldier to talk of a treaty." Little Buffalo was growing angry. He stood there and would say no more.

"Why do you come?" White Bear asked at last.

Little Buffalo was sullen. He waited long before answering. "I come to join White Bear. My heart is with him."

White Bear considered long. "We do not need Little Buffalo, or his brother Sick Wolf."

Little Buffalo took a deep, hard breath of anger.

From the darkness close by came Soldier's voice. "They turned back once. They would turn back again at a worse time."

"Go, Little Buffalo," White Bear said.

So angry that he stumbled and made great noise at the edge of the water, Little Buffalo went away.

Soldier and White Bear went silently to join the rest of the band. This place by the Animas was unclean. They would not stay the night.

"He was an enemy once. Now he is a great enemy," Soldier said.

It was so, White Bear thought.

When the leaves were dying on the trembling trees, Running Wolf came to find them. They saw him from afar and knew who he was, but for three days they played with him, letting him almost find them, then slipping away. He knew they were there, but he would not call out to them even when he knew they were close and watching him. Running Wolf played the game.

Then one day on the Villecito he built a great fire in a sand pit by the water and roasted whole a fat buck. The smell of it came back into the trees where the band was watching. They had not suffered from hunger, but it had been long since they had seen a feast like that.

Saguache's stomach began to make bear noises. The others laughed, but they were licking their lips.

"We have played long enough," White Bear said.

They joined Running Wolf then. He seemed surprised to see them, and asked where they had been all summer. "If my brothers are hungry, there is a little meat."

Ai, they were hungry. Quivera and Twin Buck were the first to throw the meat from their teeth and wash their mouths with water. White Bear held his face without expression and kept eating long after he knew the roasted buck had been smeared with the leaves of the bitter stink plant, so that not even a starving Arapahoe could have eaten it. At last, when his nose and stomach could no longer stand it, he ran for the river.

Running Wolf whooped.

They rolled Running Wolf in the sand, and then they threw him in the river. He was well recovered from the wound the red one had given him at the lake of the black rocks, for he took Soldier and Twin Buck into the water with him.

It was good to have Running Wolf with them again.

Saguache found the second deer hidden in the trees. It was even fatter than the first, and not foul from bitter stink leaves. They had a feast and much good talk of what had happened that summer, and Saguache fell asleep in the middle of boasting of the white faces he had killed.

But as always the fear of what was happening to the Utes came back to them.

"Arrow and the other chiefs have returned from the great white lodge," Running Wolf said. "Arrow now wears a shirt like the white faces. They brought back many presents."

"Did they put marks upon the talking leaves?" White Bear asked.

"Even Shavano. The talking leaves say now that all across the mountains is the white man's, even the big park where the buffalo were once like the grass in numbers."

"And no more white faces will come across the mountains?" Soldier asked.

"They say it," Running Wolf said. "The bad voice called Shallow, who returned with Arrow, said it before the council."

"Who believes it?" White Bear asked.

"Not Jingling Thunder," Running Wolf said. "Not Shavano. Shavano sits much with clouds upon his face, and sometimes will not talk, even to Arrow."

"Shavano made his mark upon the talking leaves. That means nothing. Let him council was, instead of sitting in silence in his lodge," White Bear said.

"The war chief is wise," Running Wolf said. "He is not afraid of white faces, but perhaps he sees things in his medicine that we do not see."

"Shavano is old," Jorno said. "That is all. There were eight of us this summer. We made the white faces fear to stay on this side of the mountains. Let Shavano come to our help with all the Utes who are not afraid and the white faces cannot send an army across the mountains. Let Arrow stay with his white brothers and wear their clothes."

It was good talk, true talk. But White Bear was uneasy. Even in the warm sun of the falling leaves a bad spirit came to him, and gave him a little chill like the snowbird walking on his grave. It was very bad that the Utes were divided, worse that on the side of the white faces was a wise and powerful chief like Arrow. White Bear was a little afraid of Arrow, and he knew it.

"One day Arrow will kill Jingling Thunder, like he did Red Shirt and Bad Nose when they stood against him," Running Wolf said somberly. "Jingling Thunder speaks openly against what Arrow is doing."

"Then I will kill Arrow," Soldier said.

"And then the white faces will say that Little Buffalo or Sick Wolf is chief of all the Utes, and that they will make their talk only through one of them." Running Wolf shook his head.

It was a bad thing to think about. It made them all cloudy of face, except Saguache, who had wakened and was eating again. It was even too much to hold in the head, so that night they moved again and went in search of white men.

Over one range of mountains at the hot waters near the booming rocks, they found a camp of six white faces who had built a little lodge of logs near where they had been digging in the mountain.

The band crept down through the trees to watch. One of them was careless, making a small noise or showing himself, because a white man came from behind the log lodge where he had been watching, and made the signs of peace, even though he could not see them then.

It was the same huge white face who had fought them like a bear before he escaped.

Soldier raised his rifle carefully.

"No," White Bear said. "He knows the old signs. I will talk to him."

"He was warned to go away once," Soldier said. "I will kill him."

White Bear pushed Soldier's rifle down. "There are others with him. He is a brave one, even if he is a white face."

"Soon you will be like Arrow," Soldier said angrily.

It was well that he was White Bear's great friend, but even so White Bear was still trembling with anger when he went down alone to talk to the white face. The man knew all the signs, and he spoke White Bear's language without hesitation.

"I am Big Buffalo."

"I am White Bear."

"Big Buffalo's party will stay here till the new leaves come. Arrow has said it. Your uncle, Jingling Thunder, was beside him when Arrow said it. Jingling Thunder did not like it, but he sent this to make it true."

The white man took a ring from a pouch of his clothing and held it out.

It was Jingling Thunder's ring, stripped from the finger of a Navajo in a fight before White Bear was born. White Bear did not stare too long. He tried to keep the sickness from his face. Arrow's word to all white men was different from his word to one white man, for then a chief's promise was the promise of all Utes with good hearts.

White Bear was confused. He did not know what to say.

221

"I will take council," he said, and turned back toward the hill.

He was almost to the trees when Big Buffalo shouted. White Bear turned his head to look. He saw in the door of the log lodge the red one he hated, and the red one had a rifle in his hands, already raised. It spoke while Big Buffalo was springing toward him.

White Bear's head became full of the sky. He knew no more.

On great wings White Bear came down and down until all was black, and then he soared again, and his head was full of noises of the old spirits of the mountains talking to him. He was dead, and his friends had put him in the rocks without his pony or his weapons. And now he could not ride or hunt. Then the spirits went away and his eyes were seeing other things.

He was on dead leaves in a camp. Soldier was there with him. From somewhere there came the sound of rifles.

"I am with you, brother," Soldier said. "White Bear went far toward the great hunting grounds in the sky, but now he is back once more."

White Bear listened to the rifles. "We are killing the white faces?"

"We are trying," Soldier said. "For three suns we have tried, but they are strong fighters and wise. They fight from their wooden lodge. We cannot reach them, and last night the one called Big Buffalo slipped away in the darkness. We have tried to roll the mountain

222

down upon their lodge, but it is near a ledge and our stones bounce high and go over it."

White Bear sat up. His head was loose upon his neck, and there was a tear along the side where the red one's bullet had passed.

Bit Buffalo would go to Arrow. It was best to kill the other white men as quickly as possible. White Bear did not feel like killing anything at the moment, but he got up, holding to a tree.

Killing the white men proved very difficult. The logs of their lodge were green and large and stopped bullets. The roof was of dirt. As Soldier said, rocks rolled down the mountain always struck the ledge and bounded clear beyond the lodge, which was built with one corner over a little spring.

Bit Buffalo himself must have selected the site, White Bear thought.

On the second day after he came from his sleep, White Bear took his men away. Before they faded into the mountains, they saw the dust of a large band of Arrow's warriors on a far ridge in the valley. *Ai*, Arrow was truly on the side of the white faces now.

The band spent the winter among their brother on the White River. Old Broken Knife, the chief, treated them with honor, and the young men treated them as great warriors. Soldier admitted that they were great warriors, and made free with the unmarried women.

Several times Arrow sent messengers to Broken Knife, with word to hold the band for punishment, but each time the scouts knew in advance, and White Bear was warned, so that he could take his warriors, away. And then Broken Knife had his own young men search furiously for them until the messengers would leave.

When the spring grass came and the ponies began to get the looseness from their bellies, White Bear married Gray Bird, the youngest daughter of Broken Knife. Broken Knife had held out long against White Bear's marrying his oldest daughter, Wind Eater, who had a sharp, prying voice and not much roundness to her body, but in the end he grunted that young men were all alike, and gave Gray Bird to White Bear.

By then Soldier and Jorno had returned from the San Juans with the cache of white men's rifles and ammunition hidden the summer before. Broken Knife was happy.

White Bear was happy, too, although he soon discovered that, while Gray Bird's voice was not as sharp as her sister's, it was just as prying. But she was a joy in the lodge, and her mother had taught her well about the things a warrior must have in his stomach.

CHAPTER
FIVE

Almost fifty young men wanted to go with White Bear and the others that Summer. White Bear did not want so many, but he could not well refuse, and so the young Utes made ready once more to kill all white men who crossed the mountains and who would not take the warning to leave.

Then Jingling Thunder came to the White River camp. He looked as if the winter had sat heavily on him and brought him many years all at once.

"Arrow's heart has changed toward White Bear and the other young men," Jingling Thunder said.

There had been long ceremonies and greetings with Broken Knife and the other chiefs, but now White Bear and Soldier had Jingling Thunder in White Bear's lodge.

Gray Bird left quietly to visit with the women when she saw there would be much smoking and serious talk.

Jingling Thunder watched her go with wise eyes. "Will there be a son in the month of deep snows?" he asked.

White Bear said he did not know.

Jingling Thunder's eyes twinkled. "Which, then, of Broken Knife's young men does know?"

Soldier rolled on his robes with laughing.

Jesting went soon from Jingling Thunder's eyes. "Arrow has changed his heart toward White Bear's band. There will be no punishment. Arrow sends word to return to his camp."

"What changed his heart?" White Bear asked.

Jingling Thunder smoked slowly. "Perhaps knowing that many young men are anxious to follow White Bear now. How can Arrow be chief of all the Utes if his young men do not obey?" He passed the pipe to White Bear.

"Should we obey, my father?" White Bear asked.

Jingling Thunder's eyes went far away. They saw the old campfires of the Black Indians. They saw the buffalo on the great hunting park now lost. They saw many things, and they came back to the lodge, old and troubled. "What you have done is well. You held your promise to warn all white men. The one called Rickey . . . Big Buffalo . . . spoke with a true tongue about the fight at booming rocks, and of the first time you sent him from the Ute country." Jingling Thunder was silent for a long time. White Bear passed the pipe to Soldier. "The one with the red hairy face . . . Youman . . . spoke with the forked tongue. Now I wish I had killed him when he rode past me the evening of the fight at the lake of the black rocks, but I lay hidden in the rocks and let him and the others go."

"Your arrow would have been good," White Bear said. "He is the one who killed Big Elk long ago."

Jingling Thunder turned his head slowly. "You are sure?"

226

"I am sure."

Soldier grunted. White Bear had never said before why he hated the red one so much.

Jingling Thunder stored the thought somewhere deep inside him, saying no more of it. "White Bear and my other son have killed many white faces. I do not speak against it, but can you drink the waters from the rivers, or gather all the fallen leaves from the trembling trees?"

"We can kill those who come across the mountains," Soldier said, passing the pipe around to his father.

"They will come again," White Bear said. "They are like the ones with madness in their heads when they see the yellow stones."

"*Ai,*" Jingling Thunder said. "They will not stop. I have counseled war against them. Only to White Bear and Soldier have I spoken the thoughts that come to me when the lodge is dark. Can we hold them from crossing the mountains?"

Soldier rose and made the death signs with his hands. "Let all the Utes fight together and even those who wear the striped pants and carry the long knives at their sides cannot cross the mountains."

For a time the clouds left Jingling Thunder's face and he was a fierce, hard warrior, but the doubt returned and he let the pipe go cold in his mouth. "Many follow Arrow," he said.

"We do not," White Bear said. "We will not go back."

"When I was very young," Jingling Thunder said, "my friends argued about what a bear does in his den. We did not know. To find out Jingling Thunder crawled into a den to see what the bear did."

227

White Bear and Soldier looked sidewise at each other. Jingling Thunder rose and left the lodge.

And so it was that White Bear, taking his wife, led the band back toward the summer camp of Arrow a few suns after Jingling Thunder left. With them went more than forty of Broken Knife's young men, not interested in knowing what the bear did in his den, but hoping there would be fighting against the white man later in the summer.

White Bear led them the long way, taking time to look upon all the places where the white faces had dug the summer before. They did not find a white man in the country.

Broken Knife's young men, already proving hard to handle, were disappointed.

This time Arrow's camp was at the old place below Puerta de Pocha in what by treaty was white man's country. On the way, Soldier and White Bear cast hard looks at seeing many log lodges built in green valleys since the summer before. The tame, skinny cattle of the white faces were already on the land.

"When the new white faces hear of the tall grasses of the Crooked River . . . ," Soldier said, and was then grimly silent.

The camp was like a bubbling pot when scouts brought the news that White Bear's band was returning. Young men came racing out on their ponies. They looked with envy on the scalps that White Bear's warriors wore.

White Bear and the others rode into camp with their faces straight, as if they were returning from a little hunting trip. The maidens watched them boldly. Children bounded across the grass to run beside their ponies. The chiefs watched without expression.

Sick Wolf and Little Buffalo sat beside their uncle's lodge with their faces dark, and Arrow did not come from his lodge at all, like a chief who is too great to look on small things.

Big Shavano, the war chief, came to White Bear before he was dismounted. "It is better not to show so freely the scalps of the white man," he said, while his eyes were counting.

Soldier said: "I do not see the shirt of the white faces on your back. Is it on your words?"

The thunder of his rage rolled behind Shavano's eyes. "You are on the wrong side of the mountains with your scalps."

"Your mark on the talking leaves helped make it so," Jorno said. "Where are your presents from the white chief?"

Shavano reached to pull Jorno from his pony, but White Bear was quick and sent his pinto between them, saying to Shavano: "You are right, Shavano. We will put the scalps from sight."

The war chief stalked away.

The incident put a little cloud upon White Bear's return.

Big Buffalo, the white man, came from Arrow's lodge, grinning when he saw White Bear's band. He came to them, his face changing a little when he saw the scalps, but his signs and words were good.

"White Bear and his brothers are good fighters."

229

"You are fast among the rocks," Jorno said, and laughed.

Big Buffalo laughed, too. "It is well that I was, Streak-In-The-Sky."

Jorno considered the name. He liked it.

"I was not fast enough to stop Youman from firing at your back, White Bear," Big Buffalo said. "I did not like that."

White Bear smiled. "Did White Bear like it?" And then he thought that he was making friends with a white face, so he put his features back in stern cast and rode away, but Jorno and Saguache stayed longer to talk to Big Buffalo.

Arrow waited three days before he called the council. White Bear's band had the word of Jingling Thunder that there would be no punishment, but Arrow let them wait.

Under many skins that turned away the weeping sky the council was held at a big fire at night. It seemed to White Bear that there was a little fat upon Arrow now, as on one who sits in the lodge too much, not riding to make war or hunt. But Arrow's face was the same, hard and watchful, with the same old wisdom. *Ai*, it was hard to tell about the bear, even after crawling into his den.

Arrow talked much, doing almost all the talking. He was getting like the white faces, who did not know that there must be long waiting and ceremony, even when there was little to say.

"Our young men have returned from the war trail," Arrow said. "It is well. We will need them soon."

Now even the children at the edge of the willows were listening, but Arrow did not at once continue with his thought. "White Bear's warriors have kept the white men from the Spanish Mountains. Arrow did not like the way it was done, but it is done, and there will be no punishment. Now the great white chief has said that no more of his people will cross the mountains."

Soldier started to speak, but his father jabbed him in the ribs with his elbow.

"In the month of falling leaves Arrow said that the white man, Big Buffalo, and his party could stay the winter in Ute land. It may be so again with others if Arrow says. We do not want the rocks of the mountains . . . we do not want the yellow stones of the rivers. So that there may be peace Arrow will sometimes let white men go to see about these worthless stones.

"Our young men" — Arrow looked hard at White Bear's band — "must leave those few white men to dig in peace."

"A few," Soldier muttered. "They will be like the fish of a beaver pond in numbers. They will build their log lodges, kill the game . . ."

Sick Wolf tapped Soldier lightly with a club. With him was Little Buffalo and others of the police that saw there was order at council. In the old days those with clubs rarely had anything to do but drowse in the darkness beyond the firelight, but now White Bear saw that there were many of them.

But still a man had a right to speak in council. After a while White Bear would speak.

231

Arrow went on and on. He used his own name much. He did not, as in other days, pause to ask advice of the other chiefs and the old men. But his words ran out at last.

White Bear rose to speak. Before he could say anything Arrow was talking once more.

"I am glad White Bear and his band have returned with so many strong warriors from our brother, Broken Knife. We go at tomorrow's sun to fight a great band of the Tattooed Breasts who have come into the mountains to kill our game."

White Bear never had a chance to speak. There were grunts and much shouting, with preparations for a war dance being made at once.

With his face gleaming like the black stones of the booming rocks, old Jingling Thunder said: "Many days ago Arrow knew about the Arapahoes. He knew when they were in a place where we could have caught them in the rocks, and Shavano wanted to. But Arrow waits until he could use them to keep you silent."

"I will not go to fight the Arapahoes," White Bear said.

"Soldier will not go, either."

After the camp was roaring with preparations for the war dance, White Bear sat looking at the fire. Rain was falling through the smoke hole in the hides above. Little by little it would make ashes of the bright flames in time.

The fire was the Ute Indians. The little drops coming steadily were the white faces.

Both Soldier and White Bear went to fight the Tattooed Breasts. They had to, for the young men clamored for them to go, Saguache, Twin Buck, Jorno, and the rest adding their voices. How could White Bear expect Arrow's people and the others to follow him against the white faces later if it seemed he was afraid to fight Arapahoes now?

Shavano led. He did not like it because Arrow had used his knowing of the Arapahoes to get his way in council, meanwhile letting Tattooed Breats move freely. Even though the treaty of the talking leaves said this was white face land now, still the Arapahoes had no right to be here.

Jingling Thunder said gloomily: "The white men do not care if the Indians kill each other. If they all killed each other, the white faces would be pleased."

He was so long of face that Soldier laughed at him, but Jingling Thunder did not laugh.

They rode in one day to where the scouts were watching the Arapahoes. It was not a good place for attack. To start, it was a place of ghosts, at the hill where the Utes had killed a large party of Spanish miners many long years ago. There in the rocks was still buried the muleskin bags of yellow stones and dirt the Spanish miners had been carrying with them. Then, the hill was like an old buffalo bull driven from the herd, all by itself on a flat place by the river, but close enough to the hills behind it so that the Arapahoes hunting back there had come out quickly before the Utes arrived.

Shavano scowled, and White Bear knew his thoughts — warriors could not creep upon the Arapahoe camp,

233

because there was only flatness all around the hill there on the other side of the river.

The Arapahoes rode back and forth upon their ponies, waving lances that bore Ute scalps, shouting insults across the river. There were more than 100 in their camp.

"Coyote leads them," Shavano said. "I would like to catch him in the rocks someday."

"We had the chance," Jingling Thunder said, "but Arrow waited. Now?"

"First, we will let the wild young men grow tired, so they will listen later," Shavano said.

Hot young warriors had already crossed the river farther up, among them most of those who had come with White Bear from Broken Knife's camp. They rode down on the Arapahoes in a great cloud of dust, some firing arrows and guns before they were in range.

Coyote came streaking out and counted coup with his stick on a Ute, then spun his pinto, and went back untouched.

Except for that no one went too close. The Arapahoes raced their ponies and fired their guns and arrows and made great dust. The Ute young men did the same, but no one got too close. And no one on either side was hurt.

Shavano got from his pony, sat on a rock, and smoked.

Arrow and Big Buffalo rode up together to watch.

CHAPTER
SIX

Toward evening, when most of the young Utes had come back across the river to eat and boast, White Bear and his band crossed over. Most of the Arapahoes were in their camp by then, eating and resting.

White Bear took his men straight at the scouts on the north side of the hill. Four times White Bear fired his many-shooting gun, but he still had bullets left. Soldier and the others did not fire at all. They merely whooped and made big clouds of dust smoke with their ponies.

When it was time to turn back at the safe place, the Utes did not turn. They went in faster, no longer whooping, their rifles ready. The fifteen Arapahoe guards were caught by surprise. Their ponies were tired. They had not expected anything like this on the first day of battle.

Before they realized, the Utes were very close to them, not trying to count coup, just coming in to kill them. White Bear's band rode right through them, killing two. They did not stop even then. Straight at the Arapahoe camp they rode.

The Tattooed Breasts leaped up from their cooking fires, spilling their meat in the sand, shouting angrily as they ran toward their ponies. And then White Bear turned his warriors and rode toward the high bank of the river. They slid their ponies down through the rolling white stones, crossed the river, and rode up the other bank. Arrows whacked among the choke-cherry bushes, and bullets dug into the rolling stones.

White Bear's band got up the bank and out of range.

It was a great victory, and the joke was greater yet, for they had caused the Arapahoes to become excited like squaws.

All the Ute young men rode back and forth on their side of the river and shouted insults. The Tattooed Breasts returned to their cooking fires, this time leaving many guards around their camp.

Even Shavano smiled a little. "*Ai*, that was good."

"It was good," Arrow said, but he did not smile.

That night some of Coyote's men stole across the river and killed a Ute scout and got away.

The fighting would last about three days, Jingling Thunder said. By then the Arapahoes would have had enough and be ready to leave, and the Utes would be ready to let them go.

White Bear went to Shavano with his plan. The war chief listened well, and said: "It is a way to be killed."

"It is a way to make a great victory."

Shavano thought a long time. "We will try it."

When the sun was high the next day White Bear and his band, with twenty picked young men, crept up under the high bank from far downriver, where they had gone the night before. It would not have done to go by darkness directly under the bank before the Arapahoe camp, because the Tattooed Breasts would scout in the morning to see that no Utes were hiding there.

White Bear was almost in position. From the flats above he heard the shouting and the noise where the Utes were riding in force all around the hill, keeping the enemy busy. The plan was for White Bear's warriors to rush on foot through the camp and gain the rocks behind. They would cut loose the spare ponies hidden there, then be able to fire upon the Arapahoes from their own fort.

Shavano's two large groups of warriors on the flats would close in on the north and south. The fighting would be broken then, the Arapahoes scattering, and, since the Utes outnumbered them almost three to one, there should be a great killing of Tattooed Breasts.

Like smoke from a lake in morning, two Arapahoes rose from the willows ahead, so close that White Bear could see the pigment of their war paint.

Jorno, who never left his bow behind even when he had his rifle, shot one of the Arapahoes through the throat. Saguache got the other with an arrow in the chest, then ran and killed him while the Arapahoe was struggling up the bank. The warrior had shouted, but not loud enough to be heard on the flats above.

White Bear took his young men in a rush over the bank. The new ones made loud war shouts at once, although White Bear had said not to do so until they were seen. It made little difference, for they were seen at once. Like the wind they ran to catch up with Jorno, who was far ahead in a short time.

237

Eight or nine Arapahoes who had been circling the hill came at them on their ponies. The Utes killed three of the ponies, not stopping to kill one of the riders who had been thrown and could not rise. The other Tattooed Breasts picked up their unhorsed brothers and split away, going toward the flanks of the hill for help.

Shavano's two groups feinted mighty charges, keeping most of the Arapahoes busy. And so it was White Bear's band that rushed into the camp. They found three wounded and two warriors who were trying to make a broken rifle work again. In seconds the Utes cut them dead and rushed on up the hill, where they cut loose and stampeded fifteen horses that a boy was guarding.

The young boy could have escaped, but he tried to fight. His orangewood bow was too big for him. It was clumsy in the rocks. Twin Buck killed him with a bullet.

"We have won!" Soldier shouted.

White Bear looked from the rocks, now that there was time. They had much to do yet, and nobody had won. On the north he saw Shavano trying hard to make his warriors close on the Tattooed Breasts. Shavano was doing well.

On the south the other mounted Utes were holding back, making feints, but not riding too close. White Bear saw Sick Wolf's big buckskin, and after a while he saw Little Buffalo's Grulla pony, and in a moment he could tell from the way the warriors acted that Arrow's nephews were leading the second group.

Ai, that was bad. Arrow himself must have ordered Shavano to let his nephews lead. Shavano would have sent Jingling Thunder, or Querno — or a good fighter.

Groups of Arapahoes began to break off from those opposing Sick Wolf and the others. They came back toward the hill. Arapahoes from the east side of the hill began to come down through the rocks. White Bear's men were busy soon.

Shavano made great charges, sometimes driving those before him almost to the hill before having to turn back. But the Tattooed Breasts came in from the west side now. They were no longer scattered, and they were hard to fight, as always.

Still, Arrow's nephews did not press hard. They made a show. They rode and fired their guns and shot their arrows. From across the river it would seem that they were doing well, but from where White Bear was, they were not doing well. Unless their leaders took them in, the warriors could not be expected to go within knife distance of their enemies.

The Tattooed Breasts soon saw they were not facing good leaders on the south. Many of them rode back to the hill, and began to creep up through the rocks. Soon Sick Wolf and his brother were being held off by half their number.

White Bear's band was being smothered, the Arapahoes firing now from all sides. Twin Buck was killed through the head when he rose to fire. Three others were dead.

Through the swirl of dust on the flats White Bear saw Jingling Thunder racing toward Sick Wolf's warriors,

239

with Arapahoes trying to catch him. Jingling Thunder's pony was good. The old Ute reached Sick Wolf, sitting high on his pony, waving his rifle, trying to get Sick Wolf to lead a good charge.

Sick Wolf would not do it. He wanted to council. This, White Bear could tell from the hill, although he heard nothing but the guns of the Arapahoes around him, and the bubbling of Quivera, who was dying with a bullet in the stomach and an arrow in the chest.

Jingling Thunder led a charge himself, with some of Sick Wolf's warriors following him, farther toward the hill than any had gone before from the south. The young men turned back when two were shot from their ponies.

Jingling Thunder did not turn back. He rode into the Arapahoes, striking with the rifle Soldier had given him clearing a way. He went through and to the hill, and then he rode his pony up the hill as far as the rocks would let him. And then he ran with the Tattooed Breasts rising around him.

White Bear, Soldier, and Jorno went to help. The white wings of death brushed them. Soldier killed a chief with his own knife. White Bear used his rifle like a war maul, and Jorno — Streak-In-The-Sky — was many places at once, striking with his knife. The Arapahoes had caught a great bear in Jingling Thunder. He came through them with an arrow in his thigh, and bleeding on the arms where knives had struck him. With those who came to help him, he reached the place where White Bear's group was growing smaller.

240

When Jingling Thunder had air to speak, he said: "White Bear's men must go back. Sick Wolf and his brother will not fight, and Shavano cannot fight on two sides of the hill at once."

It was so, and White Bear knew it.

Shavano knew it, too. He led all his warriors in a brave charge clear to the foot of the hill when he saw White Bear's group retreating, and before him he drove some of the Arapahoe ponies that had scattered on the flats. Fleet Jorno caught one, and then he rode and grabbed the war rope of another, and whirled it back to Jingling Thunder. It was all dust and shouting.

White Bear was knocked without wind by a pony that ran wildly. Soldier picked him from the ground. "I am with you, brother."

The Utes who had rushed the hill went back to the river, some on ponies they had caught, some still on foot. Soldier and White Bear had to go on foot, dodging Arapahoes and Utes alike. In the dust and noise it was hard to tell what was going on.

Running Wolf was wounded again. Saguache was knocked without sense by an Arapahoe lance, but Tomichi carried him away.

And still Arrow's nephews did not lead their warriors in to help, although some of the young men came by themselves and fought well.

It was enough. The Arapahoes took their dead and began to ride back into the hills. Some of the young Utes followed, hoping there would be stragglers, which there never were when the Tattooed Breasts retreated from Ute country.

Soldier and White Bear, their wounds still bleeding, the dust still in their teeth, went to find Sick Wolf and Little Buffalo. They called Arrow's nephews cowards, and pulled them from their ponies and would have killed them, but Shavano was there. With the help of other chiefs he separated the struggling fighters.

"Enough are dead," he said.

The Utes had lost almost twenty warriors. They had killed more than that number of the Arapahoes, but it was not a great victory as it should have been, and there would be terrible wailing of the women in the Ute camp on return.

Sick Wolf and Little Buffalo got up from the dust where Soldier and White Bear had left them gasping for wind.

"It was a foolish plan that White Bear made," Little Buffalo said. "He gave us many dead because of it."

The chiefs had a hard time holding White Bear.

On the slow ride back to the camp among the cottonwoods at Puerta de Pocha, Arrow looked sidewise at White Bear and said: "*Ai*, it was a foolish plan."

"It was a good plan," Shavano said. He looked fully at Sick Wolf and Little Buffalo, both unwounded.

Arrow did not say more, but his face was full of thinking as he glanced again at White Bear and Soldier.

White Bear was more wounded than he thought. It was many suns before he felt like riding on the war trail again. Many young men wanted to follow him now. Every day scouts rode in to say that white faces were crossing the mountains all the time, more and more of them.

Arrow said that he would make talk with the messenger of the white chief soon about this thing.

And then the soldiers came up the valley with the cattle, presents for the Utes. Riding at the head was the soldier, Menzies.

White Bear's insides became rocks and his brain screamed with rage when he saw who rode beside Menzies. The hairy face called Shallow — and the red one. Arrow came and stood before White Bear.

"They come in peace. Remember well, White Bear. Arrow says it."

White Bear turned away without speaking. Sick Wolf and Little Buffalo were looking at him with hatred in their eyes.

"Does White Bear go away because he fears the one called Youman will knock him over a rock again and take the knife from his hand?" Little Buffalo jeered.

White Bear made ready to leave the camp. Tomorrow he would return to the war trail against the white faces, sending Gray Bird to her father, taking with him only Soldier, Jorno, Saguache, Running Wolf, Tomichi, and Wounded Bull — those who had made the band the summer before. Quivera and Twin Buck were dead.

Jingling Thunder came to the lodge where White Bear sat staring at a cold fire pit. Gray Bird looked at the old Ute's face and went away quietly.

"The white man's cattle are lean," Jingling Thunder said. "They are like the deer that has long carried an arrow in his belly. Some of them could not even live to get here."

"White man's presents."

"Ai." Jingling Thunder smoked. "The red one talks much to Arrow. He talks of taking not one but many parties across the mountains. Arrow waits. He has made promises to Big Buffalo about the same thing, and the one called Youman is angry."

"Let the red one wait," White Bear said. "Soon Arrow will tell all white faces to cross the mountains."

Jingling Thunder looked around the lodge and saw the signs of moving. "You go?"

"I go."

"Jingling Thunder will go with you. It is time for even the old ones to fight the white faces beyond the sunset mountains. Jingling Thunder has seen the white man's presents, and they are like his work . . . lean and worthless."

White Bear's heart was glad. He said gravely: "My father is welcome. He has the strength and wisdom of ten warriors."

Jingling Thunder passed the pipe. "We cannot kill the red one here."

"He will cross the mountains again. The heavy stones have put a madness in him."

Jingling Thunder sat with folded arms. "The white one called Big Buffalo . . . he is brave. His heart is good."

"If he comes alone across the mountains, it is well. If he brings many white faces with him, he is like the rest and must be killed."

244

They smoked until the pipe was dead.

White Bear went about the camp, quietly telling his band that they would leave when the next sun came. He looked at the cattle, and they were as Jingling Thunder had said, not good for Arapahoe squaws to eat. He saw Menzies and the soldiers. They were camped apart from the Utes.

He was passing Arrow's lodge when Big Buffalo came from it. And then from behind the lodge the red one came with anger on his face. He made strong words with Big Buffalo. White Bear did not know what they were, but they came from anger, and the red one used Arrow's name often.

Big Buffalo only grinned and started away. The red one grabbed his shoulder. Like the white bear of the rocks, Big Buffalo turned. His arm pointed quickly and hard, with the fingers closed. The hand went into the red one's hairy face and knocked him to the ground. He rose with his white teeth showing.

Big Buffalo's other hand pointed and the red one sat down once more. He grabbed at the short gun in his belt. Big Buffalo had one in his hand first. He spoke soft words to the red one, who got up very angry, and went into Arrow's lodge.

Big Buffalo closed one eye and grinned at White Bear, and went away making a little song. He was a strong fighter, White Bear thought, but he should have killed the red one there on the ground. Then White Bear was glad it was not so, for he was going to kill the red one someday, even if old Jingling Thunder thought *he* would do it.

Before there was light someone brought White Bear from his robes with scratching on the lodge flaps. It was Jingling Thunder who came in before the words were said.

"Big Buffalo is dead. Your knife is in his heart. Go now."

"I did not kill Big Buffalo. Someone took my knife from the lodge while the council met last night."

"It is so, but Sick Wolf has seen the knife. He has told Menzies and Shallow and Arrow. They met. Shallow said Menzies must have his soldiers take you away. Arrow agreed."

White Bear's heart was sick. "I did not kill Big Buffalo."

"Go now!"

"How do you know this thing?"

Jingling Thunder listened at the tent flap, then looked into the dark. White Bear could hear movement at the soldier camp.

"Menzies sent Greasy Grass to tell me, so I could tell White Bear. Both Menzies and Greasy Grass think that the red one killed Big Buffalo, but Shallow says the soldiers must take White Bear. And Arrow sees the chance to have the white faces hang by the neck one who stands across his path."

Ai, it was clear enough to White Bear.

They could hear the soldiers coming. Menzies had sent the warning; he could do no more now.

White Bear grabbed his rifle and went under the hides at the back of the lodge, running in the darkness toward the herd of ponies.

246

He heard Shallow shouting in his sharp voice. He heard the soldier, Menzies, and later the red one yelled something in the white face tongue. Rifles *crashed* against the night, but no one was shooting at White Bear.

He thought of Jingling Thunder and Gray Bird left in the lodge, and would have raced back, but Soldier came out of the darkness with two ponies.

"We must ride far," Soldier said, and threw the hair rope over White Bear's arm.

Behind them the camp was in an uproar.

They rode toward the sunset mountains. Never again, White Bear vowed, would he come on the side of the rocks that the white faces owned.

CHAPTER
SEVEN

Captain Menzies drank six cups of coffee for breakfast. He paced his tent in a cold rage. His men had killed two Utes.

Munro Shallow sat smoking a cigar, smiling to himself. "Sit down, Captain. No harm is done that Arrow can't patch up. What's two dead Indians?"

"You know as well as I, Shallow, that Red Youman put that knife in Bill Rickey while he was asleep. They had a fight last night over Rickey getting the edge about going into the San Juans. Youman worked with Sick Wolf and that other nephew of Arrow's. One of them got the knife for Youman. Maybe Arrow didn't know about it . . . my guess is he didn't."

"You're making a lot of guesses, Captain." Shallow lifted the coffee pot. "My God, have you drunk all of it? Arrow didn't know about it at first, but you can bet he does now. But he's satisfied. White Bear was giving him trouble. Jingling Thunder was in his way. Now White Bear is an outlaw and Jingling Thunder is dead. You should have better control over your men, Menzies," Shallow said blandly. "Shooting White Bear's squaw . . ."

Menzies turned, gray-faced with anger. He looked a long time at Shallow, so long that red began to creep alongside the man's thick sideburns.

"Shallow, Red Youman rattled those four green recruits into firing blindly into that tent, and you know it. In fact, if I had my way, I'd hang Red Youman, and hold you responsible for framing this whole thing."

"Be careful, Menzies. In the first place, you don't have the power. In the second place, you don't have the connections to be even hinting that to me. Put it in your report of this affair . . . and see what happens to those bars." Shallow rolled his cigar slowly across his tight mouth. His eyes were cold and venomous. "Don't forget, too, in your report to mention that your men were so poorly controlled they fired when a civilian yelled that White Bear was coming out with a knife. And don't forget to mention who sent Jingling Thunder to warn that lop-eared Indian. It was Greasy Grass. Who sent Greasy Grass to tell Jingling Thunder?" Shallow laughed softly. "You sort of put yourself over a barrel, Captain."

Menzies's hands were clenched into the sides of his trousers. His face had gone from gray to white, so that the blackness of his brows was startling. His speech was a trifle slurred.

"Shallow, you're the filthiest kind of slimy thing this country has to put up with. You use the Army to do your dirty work. You don't care how many troopers or how many Indians kill each other in the process, so long as each death helps you get to that gold in the San Juans. You had Bill Rickey killed, or at least you knew

249

about it. There'll be probably fifty white men killed in the San Juans because of what you did in this camp last night, but you and your kind are so stinking rotten you don't care so long as it brings the day closer when the Army will have to move in and fight the Utes."

Shallow rose. "If you perform as well as you talk, Captain, it will be a relief to have you protecting my miners in the San Juans . . . that is, if the Army hasn't thrown you out by then."

Captain Menzies moved without haste. He spun Shallow around with one hand in the collar of the man's black coat, the other clutching the seat of Shallow's trousers. He threw him through the tent door with such force that Shallow rolled over and over until he was in the ashes of a cooking fire at the feet of a startled sergeant.

Soldier and White Bear were at the old place in the valley of purple grass when Tomichi and Wounded Bull found them, bringing news that Jingling Thunder and Gray Bird were dead.

"The Arapahoes could not kill Jingling Thunder," Tomichi said. "The white faces killed him while he stood without weapons in your lodge, White Bear."

Soldier and White Bear went separate ways into the rocks. They would not show grief, even to each other.

That night the band crept in upon a camp of white face diggers in a deep cañon by the water. Four men were sleeping on the ground, and the band killed them quickly, without much noise. But there was a cave they had not known about, the mouth of it hidden by high willows.

Two rifles sent thunder from it. Tomichi went down with a heavy grunt. The rifles spoke so fast the rest of the band had to scatter, unable to take their brother with them.

When the light came, they saw Tomichi on the ground beside the dead white men, with blood on his chest. He was not dead, for his eyes moved a little and he saw White Bear and Soldier and Wounded Bull hiding in the bushes above the cave.

It was a long wait. The sun came down into the deep cañon before a white man left the cave. White Bear put his hand on Soldier's rifle. After a while the second white face left the cave. The Utes wounded them both, so that they were easily killed.

Tomichi was dead by then. It was a poor victory.

Now the band was only three. The white faces who had crossed the mountains this summer were in much larger groups than before. They stayed closer together, even when they dug, keeping their rifles with them always. But still, they sometimes grew careless. The band killed four more of them, catching careless ones in four different camps.

The white faces were everywhere this summer, with more coming day by day. White Bear remembered Jingling Thunder's gloomy words spoken in the camp of Broken Knife: *Can we keep them from crossing the mountains?*

One day the band found a camp of ten whites that had been wiped out by Utes. Later, they found Bad

Jack, a chief of the Northern Utes, with his party of twenty-five young men. Bad Jack, too, had enough of white face promises.

It was good, and White Bear felt better, but he did not stay with Bad Jack, whose young men were noisy fighters, staying in the rocks and trees, closing in on a camp only when all the white faces in it were wounded.

Again Arrow sent Querno with many fighters to bring the warring Utes from their path. Mostly Querno tried to catch Bad Jack, whose party was large. But Querno did not catch anyone. Half of his young men left him and went with Bad Jack.

Jorno, Saguache, and Running Wolf joined the band at the camp of the smoking rock. White Bear had wondered why they were so long in coming.

"The soldier, Menzies, has come again to Arrow's camp with many cattle," Jorno said. "This time they were good cattle. Menzies said he knew they were not good last time. The Utes chased the cattle and killed them like buffalo, letting them go one at a time."

Saguache shook his head. "It was not like killing buffalo. It was not good sport."

Running Wolf, who limped from his wound at Spanish Hill, said gloomily: "The buffalo are gone from our big park of grass."

It would always be our park, White Bear thought, no matter what the talking leaves said.

"Even on the plains the buffalo are almost gone now," said Running Wolf.

They were silent for a long time.

"The soldier, Menzies, knows you did not kill Big Buffalo, White Bear," Jorno said. He looked at Saguache. "He knows the red one did it, but he cannot kill the one called Youman because the white face Shallow says the word of Utes is not good."

"It was the red one who made the young soldiers fire when Jingling Thunder and Gray Bird were killed," Saguache said. "But still Shallow took the red one away and would not let Menzies do anything."

"How does Menzies know this thing?" White Bear asked.

Jorno, Saguache, and Running Wolf smiled at each other.

"Sick Wolf said the words, telling that Little Buffalo stole White Bear's knife and gave it to the red one."

White Bear stared.

"Sick Wolf and Little Buffalo went hunting," Jorno said. "It happened that we hunted in the same place that day. Sick Wolf's ears were gone when we took him to talk to Menzies afterward. Little Buffalo could not talk at all."

"He was dead?" White Bear said.

Jorno shook his head. "He was truly a forked tongue. We did it with his own knife."

"It was better than just killing him," Running Wolf said. "This way he will be known until the last sunset as one who is a liar and a coward."

"What did Arrow . . . ?" Wounded Bull began to ask.

"Arrow was gone to get more clothes and worthless presents from his white brothers." Saguache yawned. "I am hungry. Do my brothers have meat in this camp, or must Running Wolf roast another buck?"

Ai, the band was a scourge that summer, ranging far, striking silently. As in White Bear's first attack since his return, they gave no warning. The promise had been made to Jingling Thunder, and he was dead, and he had been killed by white faces without warning.

Bad Jack's warriors were very busy, too. Others came down from the Northern Utes. Some skinny Paiutes from the big red river came to help. They were not very strong fighters, but they helped put fear into the white faces. Young men slipped from Arrow's camp and crossed the mountains. All of them wanted to join White Bear's band, but he did not want a large force, so he took only Cocho, Querno's son, who was a silent fighter.

Querno gave up in disgust and went back to Arrow's camp. Only six men went back with him. The rest were fighting the white faces in little bands of their own.

Before the torch of fall touched the leaves of the trembling trees, the white faces had again been driven from Ute country. It could be that way always, White Bear thought, if the Utes would fight as they had this summer.

CHAPTER
EIGHT

A still, heavy heat lay on the San Luis Valley, and it seemed to Captain Menzies that Fort Garland was the focus point of it, with Colonel Rowland Oder's office the very needlepoint itself.

Menzies pulled his shirt away from his chest and looked through the door at the cool summits of the Sangre de Cristo Mountains. He had been too long in the Army to complain of heat or cold or anything that could not be controlled — and a lot of things that could have been controlled.

Colonel Oder handed him the order. It was from the President himself, passed down through regular channels.

... available military forces in the area ... proceed at once ... remove from Ute Indian lands ... all miners and other trespassers ...

Menzies grinned. "At last something makes sense."

"I can spare two troops, Menzies. You'll have trouble, but don't get too rough." Oder wiped his forehead with a soggy handkerchief. "Keep on the look-out for White Bear and Soldier and bring them in, too, if you can."

255

Menzies glanced again at the order. "Even now?"

"The order still stands. Our old friend Munro Shallow has seen to that. Start this afternoon, if you want to." Oder cleared his throat and picked up another paper. "Red Youman is your guide."

Menzies stared.

"Right from the War Department, Captain. It says that Youman knows every diggings in the San Juans. It says that he should prove invaluable in dealing with the miners."

"I don't want him."

"You've got him. You don't know as many politicians as Shallow does. So you'll take him, Menzies." The colonel smiled briefly. "And you'll bring him back, too. It says here that he's 'invaluable'."

Captain Menzies took his two troops past Los Pinos Agency with Red Youman riding at his side. 500 Utes loafing at the agency, waiting for rations and gifts that never seemed to come, went wild with joy when they heard the news. They had sold much of their land, and then surveyors told them that they had sold much more than the talking leaves said. There had been councils, arguments, treaties, deals, promises during the last few years.

The Utes discovered that they had not understood the treaties and the deals. The promises were not kept, and those who came to make the treaties always said later that their chief and his big council had changed things. Meanwhile, miners and farmers had kept pushing into the San Juans. Railroads had moved toward the rich basin. Mills had been built.

Only White Bear and a few small bands that fought sporadically had stood against the incursion this last summer. They had not been enough to turn the miners back. Menzies could understand the feeling of the Utes on hearing that his soldiers were now going to move the miners out.

"A damn' fool order," Youman said. "It'd make more sense if you was going down there to kill every stinking Ute that's been giving honest miners trouble."

High on the gray hills above the Crooked River, White Bear sat his pony and watched the soldiers moving in Ute land. Running Wolf was dead now. Wounded Bull was dead. Cocho had gone back to his father, badly wounded in the fighting against the white faces. Bad Jack had quit, returning to the White River where there was now a place where food was sometimes given to the Utes, with a white man there to tell them what to do.

Ai, the water had crept through all the grass now. Only White Bear's band and a few others remained. Always Arrow had given away more land, taken more presents from the white faces, counseled peace. Arrow had put a big knife in the backs of his people. Now the soldiers had come.

"Shall we fight them?" Soldier spoke without boasting. They were four. Jorno, Saguache, he, and White Bear. Soldier saw from one side of his face now. A bullet that slid upon the rocks in a fight the summer before had torn away the corner of his right eye.

257

"We will fight the soldiers," White Bear said. "Go. Tell all the young men scattered in their summer lodges to gather at the old camping place beyond the bright lake of the black rocks. White Bear will watch the soldiers."

It was the first time White Bear had ever asked for help. It was time. The sun was growing dark over what was left of Ute land.

For two days he watched the soldiers. They moved without haste. On the second day they turned in the gray sage toward the lake of the black rocks. White Bear had been seen, he knew, but it made no difference, for the one who led the striped pants was Menzies, and he would know that he was being watched.

At the place of the dying elk, when the soldiers were eating, Menzies rode alone toward the hill where White Bear was making the signs of peace. White Bear did not put down his rifle, and he let Menzies ride clear up the hill to him.

There were no more years on the soldier, it seemed to White Bear. He was as brown and straight as ever. They made all the signs, then sat upon the ground facing each other. Menzies did not use White Bear's name.

"We've come to put the miners from the Ute lands."

White Bear thought he had not heard with good ears.

"The great white chief has said it."

"It is time," White Bear said.

Menzies nodded gravely. "When you ride the country, if you see the one called White Bear, tell him that Arrow and the white chief still are angry with him.

Tell White Bear to stay hidden in the mountains. Perhaps in time the anger against him will pass."

"I will tell him," White Bear said.

He watched Menzies ride back to the camp. Why did one who spoke with a true tongue let the red one ride with him? Right now the red one, who had watched with the far-seeing glasses, was shouting at Menzies, pointing toward the hill. He shouted in his anger so loudly that White Bear heard his own name.

Menzies's heart was good, but still the soldiers must be watched to see that it was so about putting the miners from the San Juans. White Bear, who knew all that had happened in many councils, even though he had not been there, knew that the white faces sent to speak to the Utes said one thing with good heart — and then later their big chiefs clamed another thing had been said. *Ai*, it would be well to watch the soldiers.

Before the sun was gone, Jorno and Saguache came to say that 300 fighters would be gathered at the lake of the black rocks that night, almost all of them with guns.

It was hard for White Bear to say: "The soldiers come to make the white face miners leave our lands. The one called Menzies has said it."

Jorno and Saguache would not believe at first.

"Until we see if this thing is true, we will not fight," White Bear said.

They watched a white soldier coming fast on his horse to catch the troops, now moving across the little valley of many bucks. This last one had come many far miles, for his horse was wobbling. He rode to Menzies and gave him a talking leaf. All the soldiers stopped.

After a while the red one made a great booming sound of laughing that came faintly to White Bear and the others on the hill.

The soldier put their horses out to grass. Presently Menzies, looking all around, signaled the hill where White Bear was. They rode toward it.

This time White Bear went down to meet him.

Great anger and shame was on the face of Menzies, but he made all the signs, not speaking quickly like an excited squaw.

"The great white chief has changed his mind. We are not to put the miners from the San Juans."

After a while the soldiers rode back the way they had come.

For a long time the three Utes sat on the hill with bitterness eating at their hearts. Then Jorno said: "I will ride to watch the soldiers, to see that they are not tricking us again."

White Bear and Saguache went to the old camping place above the lake of the black rocks. Nearly 400 warriors were there, and they were ready to fight. Soldier wanted to take them after the striped pants and kill them all, including Menzies. It made no difference to Soldier that Menzies had been told what to do by his chief. Many young men grunted in agreement when they heard Soldier's angry speech.

"They go," White Bear said. "Let them go."

"Then they will return to guard the miners someday," Soldier said. "It is better to kill them now."

"Fighting here in the rocks, where we were ready, is not like trying to fight them in the open of the Crooked River," White Bear said. "They will be there before we can catch them." For the first time White Bear wondered gloomily if Arrow had been right in not wanting to fight the white faces.

"Something has changed White Bear's heart," Soldier said. "Does he grow afraid?"

"Menzies is taking the striped pants away," White Bear said. "Let them go."

He and Soldier quarreled bitterly. In the end, Soldier took all who would follow and rode to fight the cavalry. By then many Utes had slipped into the night, their hotness cooling after thinking how it would be to meet the soldiers in the open by the Crooked River. Saguache went with Soldier.

White Bear sat alone. It was like the night when he had sat by the fire thinking of the death of Red Cow, and it was not far from the same place. Faces moved in the flames, Red Cow, Twin Buck, Quivera, Jingling Thunder, Gray Bird, Tomichi, Wounded Bull — all gone to the sky . . .

He heard a pony coming. For a while out there in the darkness where he met it, he did not know who it was that had fallen across his moccasins.

Jorno's voice was not strong. White Bear felt a great hole in his back when he reached to help him.

"At night the red one left the soldiers and went toward the San Juans on the trail of stolen ponies," Jorno said. "I followed to kill him, but he hid beside the trail and killed me instead."

It was so. When White Bear got his brother to the fire, he saw that Jorno had not long to live. *Ai*, this day had brought great blackness.

Jorno was dead when White Bear rode the war trail after the red one. He found the first marks at daylight. Then he saw where the white man had stepped from his horse to a high rock beside the trail, and hidden to shoot Jorno when he came. The horse had gone on up the mountain, then waited in the trees for the red one to mount again. It would be a good horse to own, White Bear thought.

Twice more that day he found where the red one had tried the trick, taking no chances that others besides Jorno had not been following. White Bear would not be caught that way. On the second day he thought he knew where the red one was going, toward the big camp of the white miners in the park of snowy mountains.

White Bear cut wide to the north and rode hard to get ahead. He put many bleeding places on the legs of his pony, but the red one was still ahead when he reached the spring that never stops. White Bear's pony was used up. He changed to Jorno's buckskin, which did not like the extra weight, but it was fleet and strong.

And so on the third evening White Bear caught up with his enemy, who was camped in the rocks in a bad place to get at. He had a small fire that sent little smoke and did not show, but the smell of it came to White Bear, who waited for darkness.

After dark, there was still a little fire, which did not fool White Bear. The red one knew he was close. The red one would not be sleeping near that fire.

Very slowly White Bear went in, so well that even the red one's horse did not see or hear or smell him to give an alarm. The fire was almost dead, but it gave enough light for White Bear to see, after some time, a blanket and the stock of a rifle where the red one lay between two rocks some distance from the fire.

Fading back into the darkness, White Bear went around the camp, but not far enough to let the red one's horse catch his smell. He crept in with his knife. He was close enough.

Too late White Bear learned the trick. The red one was not where the gun and blanket lay. He was beyond, in the blackness near the horse.

The thunder was like the noise that had wakened White Bear long ago when first he heard it. Three times it came. After the first time, White Bear was lying flat on his back from a bullet that had smashed his left arm and knocked him over.

Then the red one came from the darkness as one who knows his bullets always go true. But he still had the short gun in his hand and it was ready. White Bear waited while the red one came closer, even then not making any noise.

The Ute's right arm was strong. He threw his knife so that it could not miss. The red one grunted. His gun flamed. By the light of it, while springing up, White Bear saw that his knife had gone too high. It was just under the red one's shoulder, not in his heart. But it had caused the red one to drop his gun even as he fired it.

White Bear went in to put the knife where it belonged.

The white man was like a grizzly. He tore White Bear's good hand from his throat and made the stars come down with blows against his face. He hugged him with big arms and made the bones of White Bear's back cry out. Then White Bear used his legs and knees in the way he had been taught in childhood.

It was good. They went down together with the red one underneath. White Bear felt for his knife, but it had been knocked loose from the red one's shoulder. He tried again to kill the white man with his one hand.

Youman rolled with him, and just in time White Bear remembered to keep the roll going. They went over twice, crushing out the fire. White Bear was still on top. Fingers struck his eyes and blinded him. He had to dig his head against the heavy smell of the red one's shirt to keep from losing his eyes.

Grunting curses, Youman came up with his great strength seeming to grow greater. He brought White Bear up with him, held him with one hand, hit him with the other so that all the rocks of the mountain were rolling in White Bear's head.

He held with his hand to the white man's beard and used his legs again. This time the red one crashed backward into a rock and did not fall. But much strength went from him. One hand that had been killing White Bear's wind fell away.

Ai, White Bear had him then, he thought, and tried once more to crack the red one's head against the rock.

The pain in White Bear's side was not great at first, and then the sharpness came again. The red one's hand that had gone from his throat was striking with a knife. White Bear twisted, using his legs once more. This time the red one struck the rock so that he could not move for a moment. It was long enough for White Bear to get his fingers gripped as he wanted them.

He bent his enemy across the rock with his back curving more and more, with Youman's head going lower and lower. And still the red one had great life. He almost broke the hold and flung White Bear back. But now, his strength flowing fast, White Bear was fighting everything bad that had happened to him. He held on and used his power until a dull *snapping* told him that it was done.

White Bear fell across the body and could not move for a while. He fell again when he tried to go toward his pony. For a while he crawled toward his pony. Then he could not remember where it was at all. A great blackness came to him.

As once long ago when the red one had shot him in the head, he came down and down and saw the world again. Soldier was squatting beside him.

"I am with you, brother."

White Bear's wounds had been bound with fresh hide from a pony, but it would not be enough, he knew.

"When is it?" he asked.

"Two suns after you killed the red one."

"He is dead?"

"He is dead," Soldier said.

"You fought the striped pants?"

"Only a little. Few went all the way with us. We fought them just enough that Saguache was killed. It was too much. We should have heard your words, brother."

"I have few left," White Bear said. "But my eyes are with me yet. Take me high into the rocks."

They came at last to a great tumbled place of gray slabs where the old spirits long ago had thrown stones in mighty anger.

"White Bear will stay here."

Soldier helped him to sit against a rock.

Below them the San Juans were spread with their gleaming rivers, the great gray mountains reaching toward the Manitou. They saw the valleys with their rich green grass, the cool forests of trembling trees and dark pines. It seemed to White Bear that it was safe now. It was secure forever and would always be the sacred hunting grounds where the grass never burned away or the game grew scarce.

"Go back to Arrow's camp," White Bear said. "The land is ours now till the last big sunset, and there will be no more trouble. The red one was the last to go, and it is done now."

"Soldier will go." Soldier knew that White Bear could not see the smoke of white face fires below them, or the growing scars of those who dug the mountains.

"We fought to be free," White Bear said. "Even if we had lost, it would be well." For a moment his eyes were puzzled and he looked at Soldier with fear. "We have won a great victory. That is true?"

"It is so. The white faces have been driven from our land forever, White Bear."

After a while White Bear murmured: "Running Woman . . . Running Woman, the lodge grows cold . . ."

From the mists above the vast San Juans, White Bear's grandmother came toward him, smiling. Her buckskins were like the snow, her braids shining like the wetness on the booming rocks, and she was not old.

"It is well, He Cries," she said.

Not long afterward Soldier went from the mountain alone, going toward Arrow's camp.

ABOUT THE AUTHOR

Steve Frazee was born in Salida, Colorado, and in the decade 1926–1936 he worked in heavy construction and mining in his native state. He also managed to pay his way through Western State College in Gunnison, Colorado, from which in 1937 he graduated with a Bachelor's degree in journalism. The same year he also married. He began making major contributions to the Western pulp magazines with stories set in the American West as well as a number of North-Western tales published in *Adventure*. Few can match his Western novels that are notable for their evocative, lyrical descriptions of the open range and the awesome power of natural forces and their effects on human efforts. *Cry Coyote* (1955) is memorable for its strong female protagonists who actually influence most of the major events and bring about the resolution of the central conflict in this story of wheat growers and expansionist cattlemen. *High Cage* (1957) concerns five miners and a woman snowbound at an isolated gold mine on top of Bulmer Peak in which the twin themes of the lust for gold and the struggle against the savagery of both the elements and human nature interplay with increasing, almost tormented intensity. *Bragg's Fancy Woman* (1966) concerns a free-spirited woman who is able to tame a family of thieves. *Rendezvous* (1958) ranks as one of the finest mountain man books, and *The Way Through the Mountains* (1972) is a major historical novel. Not surprisingly, many of Frazee's novels have become major motion pictures. According to the second edition of *Twentieth Century Western Writers* (1991), a Frazee story is possessed of "flawless characterization, particularly when it involves the clash of human passions, believable dialogue, and the ability to create and sustain damp-palmed suspense."

ISIS publish a wide range of books in large print, from fiction to biography. Any suggestions for books you would like to see in large print or audio are always welcome. Please send to the Editorial Department at:

ISIS Publishing Limited
7 Centremead
Osney Mead
Oxford OX2 0ES

A full list of titles is available free of charge from:

Ulverscroft Large Print Books Limited

(UK)
The Green
Bradgate Road, Anstey
Leicester LE7 7FU
Tel: (0116) 236 4325

(Australia)
P.O. Box 314
St Leonards
NSW 1590
Tel: (02) 9436 2622

(USA)
P.O. Box 1230
West Seneca
N.Y. 14224-1230
Tel: (716) 674 4270

(Canada)
P.O. Box 80038
Burlington
Ontario L7L 6B1
Tel: (905) 637 8734

(New Zealand)
P.O. Box 456
Feilding
Tel: (06) 323 6828

Details of **ISIS** complete and unabridged audio books are also available from these offices. Alternatively, contact your local library for details of their collection of **ISIS** large print and unabridged audio books.